I0775419

MOLLY'S LETTER

A TEA ROSE STORY

Jennifer Donnelly

Wild Rumpus Books
New York

MOLLY'S LETTER Copyright ©2023 by Jennifer Donnelly. All rights reserved. No part of this book may be used or reproduced in any manner whatsoever without written permission except in the case of brief quotations embodied in critical articles or reviews.

www.jenniferdonnelly.com

Cover Design: Rochelle Bolima

First Edition, October 2023

ISBN: 979-8-9886471-1-9

This one's for you, dear reader.
Thank you for never giving up on these characters,
or on me.

XO,

Molly's Letter

A Tea Rose Story

Prologue

New York City, October 1888

Death was near.

He was rattling the knob. Pounding on the door.

"Michael? Michael, it's me, Father Garrity, let me in!"

But Michael Finnegan would not fall for Death's tricks.

"Be gone, yeh bastard!" he shouted.

He'd locked the door moments ago. Now he pulled the curtains and knelt by the bed where his wife lay. He didn't look at her face; he couldn't. Instead, he lifted her hand and pressed her palm to his cheek. Her fingers felt as thin as a bundle of sticks.

"Do you want a sip of water, Molly?" he said, forcing a smile into his voice. "Your glass is right here on the night table. You'll have to sit up, though. Can you do that? Can you sit up, love?"

His words faded into the silence of the sour, airless room.

Michael released Molly's hand and made himself look at her, made himself see her wasted face, the sharpness of her bones beneath her skin. An anguished groan wrenched itself from his throat. He banged his skull against the wooden headboard, again and again and again.

"Michael! For the love of God, open the door before it's too late!"

"*No*," Michael whispered.

He stood up and started to pace back and forth, his eyes never leaving the door. A dizzying confusion gripped him. How had this happened? *How*? No matter how many times he went over it in his head, it still made no sense.

Molly had looked a little tired two days ago, even after her morning cup of tea, but what woman didn't only a month after having a baby? He'd told her to have a lie-down with Nell and that he'd clear the breakfast dishes. She'd said she would, and had taken her cookbook down off the shelf, meaning to page through it before she slept.

"We've not had a cake since Nell came along," she called over her shoulder, as she headed out of the kitchen. "I'll bake one to have with the Sunday dinner. We could ask the Munros to come."

Michael said he thought that was a fine idea. He washed the dishes, then he went downstairs to open the shop. When he returned at noon for a bite to eat, he knew something was wrong the instant he opened the door.

Nell was crying—not the loud, lusty howls she let out when she was hungry or wet but a low, whimpering moan.

"Molly?" he called, hurrying to the bedroom.

But Molly wasn't there.

The baby was in her crib. Her eyes were swollen shut from crying. Shivers racked her little body; wetness from her diaper had soaked her clothing. At the sight of her, a cold dread gripped him. Molly would never have willingly left Nell like this.

"Hush, Nell, it's all right. Daddy's here," he said, grabbing the throw at the foot of his and Molly's bed. He wrapped it around the baby, then picked her up and held her close, rubbing her back to soothe her.

"Molly?" he shouted, pounding down the hallway. "Molly, where are you?"

He hurried to the sitting room, and then the kitchen, but she wasn't anywhere to be found. Then he heard water running. He ran to the bathroom and pushed the door open.

Fear unfurled inside him like the petals of a black rose at the sight of his wife.

She had collapsed on the floor. Her eyes were closed. Sweat had plastered her nightgown to her body. The woman he'd kissed good-morning, the woman he'd eaten breakfast with, was gone. Molly, with her pink cheeks, her full-lipped smile, was *gone*. A hollow-eyed wraith had taken her place.

"Jaysus, love! What's wrong?" he cried, kneeling down to her, Nell balanced in the crook of his arm.

Molly lifted her head at the sound of his voice. Her eyes fluttered open. Her gaze was unfocused at first, but as it settled on him, and then Nell, fear spread across her ashen face.

"Get her away from me, Michael," she rasped. "I'm ill…"

The sink's cold tap was running full force; Michael could barely hear her over the noise of it. He clumsily stood to turn it off and as he did, Nell's whimpers rose to wails.

"Get Nell *away*," Molly moaned. As she spoke, a spasm shuddered through her body. She clutched her belly, keening with pain.

Michael's fear turned into terror. He backed away from her, crashing into the bathroom door, almost falling with Nell in his arms, then stumbled out of their flat to the landing. He meant to call up to Mary Munro, a widow who lived on the third floor, to send for the doctor, but Mary was already on her way down to him, worry on her face.

"I heard shouting," she said as she reached the landing. "Is everything all right?"

When Michael told her what had happened, Mary took Nell from him, heedless of whether the baby might be contagious. "I'll send Ian to fetch Dr. Mason," she said. "Help Molly. *Go.*"

Molly was barely conscious when Michael returned to her. He pulled her wet nightgown off, washed her, then carried her to their bed, telling her the whole time that she was going to be fine, trying to keep himself calm. But it was so hard; she was fading before his eyes.

Dr. Mason arrived as Michael was pressing a cold compress to Molly's forehead. After examining her, the doctor hurried to the kitchen, rolling up his sleeves as he went. He knew the flat; he'd delivered Nell. He returned a few minutes later with a basin, clean rags, a jug of water, and a rubber sheet.

"I'm worried about Nell. What if she's got what Molly has?" Michael said.

"It's unlikely. Children get this the same way adults do, through contaminated water," Dr. Mason replied.

Fear coiled around Michael's heart like a snake at the doctor's words. He knew the name of the disease that was carried in bad water, but Dr. Mason was wrong, he had to be. Outbreaks had occurred in the city all summer long, but not in their neighborhood. Their water was clean.

"Did Molly eat or drink anything unusual yesterday?" Dr. Mason asked.

"No. We ate all our meals together," Michael replied.

"Did she go anywhere out of the ordinary?"

Michael thought for a moment. "No, she —" he began, but then he remembered that Molly *had* gone somewhere and the snake inside him tightened its coils. "The Five Points," he said. "She went with the nuns. They took clothing to an orphanage."

Dr. Mason swore at the mention of the notorious slum. "There's been another outbreak in the Five Points," he said. "She must've drunk something while she was there."

"Dr. Mason, what is it?" Michael asked, still desperately pretending to himself that he didn't know.

"Cholera, Mr. Finnegan," Dr. Mason replied. "I'm sorry. I'll do everything I can for her."

He didn't say anything else. He didn't need to. Michael knew what cholera did to its victims. It was merciless, savagely dehydrating them in a matter of hours, causing their blood to thicken and their organs to fail. Most lasted only a day or two, some not even that long, before their ravaged bodies gave out.

The next few hours had been a hellish blur.

Dr. Mason had stayed by Molly's side that day and the next, trying to get water down her, trying to ease her pain and chafe away the blue tinge creeping into her hands and feet.

As dusk fell at the end of the second day, there had been a glimmer of hope. Molly had sat up and asked for paper and something to write with. Dr. Mason had dug in his bag and pulled out a notepad. He'd torn a sheet out of it and handed it to her, along with a pen. She'd motioned for the cookbook on her bedside table, and with shaking hands had scribbled something on the paper, using the book as a makeshift desk. Michael, watching anxiously from the doorway, had seen her do it.

"That's a good sign, isn't it?" he'd said a few minutes later, dogging Dr. Mason as he rushed to the kitchen once more. "She asked for her cookbook. She's planning the Sunday dinner. She'll be up soon, won't she?"

But the rally hadn't lasted. Half an hour later, the cookbook was back on the night table and Michael was hunched over in a chair in a corner, his head in his hands, as the cramps twisted Molly's limbs, making her scream with pain. As the seizures started. As she fell into a coma.

At four in the morning on the third day, Dr. Mason, gray-faced with exhaustion and sorrow, had left. "I've done all I can," he'd said, putting a hand on Michael's shoulder. "It's a priest she needs now."

Ian Munro had hurried out in the darkness to fetch Father Garrity, to give Molly last rites. But Michael, crazed by fear, had locked the bedroom door and refused to let him in.

A fresh volley of pounding carried to him now, every slam of the priest's fist against the door like a spike through his heart.

"Be gone, I said!" he shouted. "Did you not hear me?"

But it wasn't Father Garrity who answered him.

"Michael, it's me, Mary. You mustn't do this, Michael. Think of her. Think of Molly. If you love her, open the door. *Please*, Michael."

Michael covered his face with his hands. How could he do what they were asking? They might as well ask him to rip his own heart out. It was some time before he lowered his hands, and by then dawn had broken behind the closed curtains, setting them aglow. Slowly, step by stumbling step, he made his way to the window. Summoning every last scrap of his strength, he opened the curtains.

The first rays of the autumn morning, golden and soft, poured into the room. They fell across the bed, across Molly's wasted body. The light, the warmth on her face…they eased her. Her breathing slowed. A whisper of a smile passed over her parched lips.

Michael saw it, and images danced across his memory, sparkling and gossamer, images of all their beginnings. The first time he'd seen her—at a summertime party, in a white dress, laughing. And how, standing there, struck dumb by her loveliness, he'd felt that his life had been nothing, nothing at all, until that very moment. Asking her to marry him, down on one knee in the park as the skies suddenly opened. How they'd run under an oak tree for shelter, and she'd kissed him, her answer in her lips. Their wedding night, and all their nights after. Holding their newly born Nell.

He no longer knew how to live without her. How could he let her go?

Mary's voice drifted back to him. *Think of her. Think of Molly. If you love her…*

He loved her. God, how he loved her.

Michael went to his wife and kissed her lips.

Then he unlocked the door.
And let Death come inside.

Chapter 1

New York City, June 1891

Fiona Finnegan Soames took a deep breath and reveled in the quiet.

The Saturday crowd had been relentless. The clock had just struck six and she was exhausted. Her customers were gone now; her staff, too. The tearoom had been scrubbed and swept, the silver polished, the cushions plumped, and the day's earnings safely locked away.

She was standing in the back garden of her Gramercy Park brownstone by herself, yet she was not alone, for arching over the doorway, trellised along the high brick walls, and dipping gracefully over the tables, were her beloved tea roses. They were her creatures and she was theirs, and no matter how weary she was, she made a point every evening to spend a peaceful moment walking among them.

The profusion of blooms—in dusty pinks, deep reds, ivories, and soft yellows—was breathtaking, and as Fiona admired them, a gentle breeze swept down, making it look as if the flowery heads were nodding, as if they understood.

The tea roses were why Fiona had bought the brownstone, why she'd taken the immense gamble of opening a tearoom. When she'd first seen them, growing so tall in the abandoned garden, neglected and weed-choked yet flowering defiantly, they had spoken to her. They had whispered that she, too, would endure. That she would rise above the ruins of her life and bloom.

She reached up now, pulled a crimson rose to her and inhaled its beguiling scent, and for a moment she was no longer in New York, but in East London, sitting at the top of a set of stone steps. A boy called to her, a boy with a smile that promised her the world and everything in it. He handed her a single red rose.

Fiona tried to box the memory away, afraid of where it would lead her. To a sun-dappled river. To autumn air tinged with coal smoke and the scent of tea leaves. To her past, a place to which she could never return. But the memory refused to be confined. It danced down the hallways of her heart, pulling her along with it, showing her a stolen kiss. Coins in an old cocoa tin. A thin gold ring with a tiny sapphire. So many first times, and then the last time, at the lapping river's shore. Tears threatened. Fiona blinked them back and released the rose, hoping to release the ghost it had conjured as well. As she did, a voice carried out to the garden from the tearoom.

"Fee! Darling wife! Where in blazes are you?"

The voice was a man's—English, like her own, but impossibly posh. Before Fiona could answer, her husband of not quite two years, Nicholas Soames, bounded onto the terrace. At the sight of him, her sad memories faded like a cold mist in the bright morning sun. A smile spread across her face—a broad, beautiful grin that brought color to her cheeks and made her indigo eyes sparkle.

Tall, slender, and heartbreakingly handsome, Nick was wearing a cream linen suit and a sky-blue cravat. His color was high, and his blond bangs, usually neatly swept back off his high forehead, had flopped down over one eye. He was holding a bottle in one hand.

"Why do you have champagne?" Fiona asked him.

"Because we're celebrating!" he exclaimed. "We'll have a toast after supper. With Michael and Mary and Alec and Nell and the boys."

"Who are we toasting?"

"New York's most brilliant art dealer!"

Fiona craned her neck, pretending to look past him. "Where is he? I'd love to meet him."

"Aren't you funny," Nick said. He plunked the bottle down on a table, pulled her close, and whispered three words in her ear. "I sold it."

Fiona pulled back from him a little, the better to see his face. Her eyes searched his. "Sold what?"

"The Van Gogh."

Fiona's hands came up to her mouth. "Nick, you *didn't*."

The painting, *Irises*, had arrived in a crate last year with several others of sunflowers and almond trees. They'd been shipped over from France by Nick's art-dealer friend, and the painter's brother, Theo. Fiona had watched as Nick had unpacked the paintings one-by-one, and had found herself strangely drawn to them. They were raw, bold, and inexplicably moving.

"Durand-Ruel bet me a hundred dollars that I'd never sell a single canvas," he crowed now, referring to the legendary French art dealer who had been Nick's employer when he lived in Paris, and who now operated a rival gallery in New York. "I can't wait to collect my winnings. I'll buy you a bauble with them, Fee. Something bright and shiny. What would you like?"

"I'm not sure," Fiona said, her brow furrowing. She thought for a second, then snapped her fingers. "An adding machine!"

Nick's eyes widened in dismay. "How thoroughly appalling."

"How about a set of industrial scales, then? They'd make processing bulk orders of tea much more efficient."

"How about a pair of earrings?" Nick countered. "Or a pendant to dangle invitingly above your cleavage?"

Fiona snorted. "Cleavage doesn't sell tea."

"Cleavage sells everything. Now lock up, will you? We're late for supper and I'm starving," he said, ready to leave. "I hope Mary is making roast chicken tonight. And roast potatoes. With gravy and rolls and —"

Fiona caught hold of his hand, stopping him. He turned to her, his eyes questioning.

"I'm proud of you, Nicholas," she said quietly.

They liked to tease each other. About everything. All the time. But Fiona was not teasing now. She knew what success meant to Nick for she knew what it had cost him: his family, his country, the man he'd loved.

"Of course you are," Nick said breezily. "How could you not—"

Fiona cut him off. He was trying to deflect her words and the emotion underneath them—it was his way—but she would not let him. "I mean it, Nick. I'm proud of you."

Nicholas tried for a smile, but it turned into a wince. He looked down at their clasped hands, saying nothing, just twisting the gold wedding band on her finger back and forth. Then he leaned his forehead against hers and for a long moment, they stood that way, not talking, for what they felt was too deep for words.

They had met in England, as Nick was getting on a ship bound for New York and Fiona was trying to do the same—without a ticket. Nick had saved her life, and Seamie's, too, by getting them on that boat. And, later, after they'd arrived in New York and a dread disease had carried him to the brink of death, Fiona had saved his. Though their marriage was unconventional, their bond was unbreakable. They were not lovers but the truest of friends. They belonged to each other, heart and soul, and always would.

Nick was the first one to break the silence. "Let's go, old mole. Or else you'll make me blub and that won't do. New York's most brilliant, and handsomest, and wittiest, and also most stylish, art dealer cannot be seen out and about with red eyes and a snotty nose."

Laughing, Fiona led the way inside. Nick picked up his bottle of champagne and followed her. As he made his way through the tearoom, she locked the terrace doors, double-checked that the oven was off, and grabbed her shawl off the back of a chair.

"It's strawberry season. A Victoria sponge for dessert would be nice, wouldn't it?" Nick said, as Fiona locked the front door. "Slathered with jam and whipped cream? Mary is such a good baker."

"How come you never talk about my cooking so fondly?" asked Fiona, as they set off up the street.

"Because your cooking is egregious, my darling girl. That dish you made last night?" He shuddered.

"The pork medallions? They were French! *Escalope de Porc au Cognac*!"

"They were a felony."

Fiona scowled at him.

"Don't give me that look. You know it's true. You are many wonderful things, Mrs. Soames, but a cook is not one of them."

"I suppose you're right. And a Victoria sponge *does* sound awfully good."

Nicholas offered her his arm and she took it. She was still tired, her body ached from the long day, and her heart ached from her memories. But she was happy, too. Happy for Nick's success, and happy for her own. Happy for second chances. Happy, most of all, to be walking arm in arm with her husband, her best friend, through the soft summer evening and the city of their dreams.

Chapter 2

"You look so pretty, Mary!" Fiona exclaimed, kissing her friend on the cheek. "Have you dressed up just for us?"

"No, I—" Mary started to say, but Nick cut her off.

"You *did* make roast chicken!" he exclaimed, kissing Mary's other cheek. "I can smell it from here! Tell us you've made a Victoria sponge, too, and all my wishes will have come true."

"Well, I made a trifle," Mary replied, in her soft Scottish burr. "With the leftovers from yesterday's sponge."

"Close enough!" Nick said, then he bounded down the hallway, champagne bottle in hand.

Fiona shook her head in disbelief. "*Close enough?*" she called after him. "I think you what you meant to say was thank you!"

But Nick didn't hear her; he was already in the kitchen.

Fiona and Nick had just arrived at her Uncle Michael's flat, in the west side neighborhood known as Hell's Kitchen. The Finnegans and the Munros gathered to have supper there every Saturday.

"Is that a new dress?" Fiona asked Mary, as they walked toward the kitchen together. "I haven't seen it before."

"It is new, yes," Mary said, smiling at Fiona's compliment. "I'm glad you like it."

The dress was a deep pink and it set off Mary's warm brown eyes and her chestnut hair. Fiona wondered if she had worn it for Michael. She hoped her uncle noticed the dress and complimented her on it. Mary and Michael had started spending more time together over the last few months, and Fiona was certain that a quiet, but deep, affection was blossoming between them.

As they entered the kitchen, Fiona draped her shawl over the back of a chair. She greeted Alec, Mary's father-in-law, whose gray head was just visible behind an evening newspaper; Nell, sitting in her chair, a thick book under her as a booster, going on three now and the spitting image of Michael with her blue eyes and black hair; and Ian, Mary's son, almost a man at sixteen, and handsome with his mother's coloring.

Seamus, Fiona's seven-year-old brother, was standing on a stepstool at the counter mashing potatoes, his sleeves rolled up, one of Mary's aprons tied around him. Alec had picked him up after school, as he often did when Fiona and Nick could not break free from work. Fiona crossed the kitchen and kissed the top of Seamie's head.

"*Feeeeee*," he whined, ducking her.

"Don't bother the man," Nick scolded, tucking his champagne into the icebox. "Can't you see he has a job to do?"

Fiona frowned ruefully. This was a recent development. Over the past few weeks, Seamie had turned into a boy who no longer wanted anything to do with kisses and cuddles. He preferred to be out digging in the garden with Alec, hammering shelves together with Michael, or hanging paintings with Nick. He was growing up, she supposed, and she was grateful he had such good, kind-hearted men in his life to show him the way—but still, she couldn't pretend it didn't hurt. She ruffled his hair, her way of telling him that he wasn't *so* grown up...not yet.

"Seamie, put a bit more butter in those potatoes. Fiona, put these on the table, would you?" Mary asked, handing her a basket of warm rolls.

It was close and crowded in the kitchen, and Fiona had to edge around Seamie, Nick, and Ian to get to the table, but nobody minded. They were happy to be eating together in the cheerful, cozy kitchen, even on a warm evening.

As she put the rolls down, Fiona noticed there were only seven place settings, not eight. She glanced around and saw that her uncle was missing. "Where's Michael?" she asked.

"I don't know," Mary replied. "But it's not like him to miss roast chicken."

As if on cue, they all heard the flat door open and close, and a moment later Michael joined them.

"Sorry I'm late," he said, giving Nell a kiss. "Door on the blasted meat cooler got stuck again. Took me longer than I thought it would to fix it."

"We'll need one more place setting," Fiona said. "I'll fetch it."

"There's no need, Fiona. I won't be eating with you this evening," Mary said, setting a platter of cut-up chicken on the table.

Fiona turned to her, puzzled. Mary always ate with them. "Why not?"

"I'm attending a concert at the Union League Club."

Alec lowered his newspaper. "A concert? At a club?" he echoed, in a tone that suggested Mary might as well have said she was heading over to the Bowery to catch a burlesque show.

Michael, washing his hands in the sink, turned to look at her, his forehead creased with concern. "You're going out at night all by yourself?"

Mary met his gaze. "No, I'm going with a friend."

"Well, that sounds like fun," Nick said.

"Who is she?" Michael asked, drying his hands on a dish towel.

Mary hesitated, then she leveled her chin and said, "He."

The room fell into a shocked silence. Even Nell, happily sticking her finger in the butter, went quiet.

Fiona, Alec, and Michael all found their voices at the same time. "*He*?" they said in unison.

"You never told us about a he," said Nick.

"I didn't realize I was required to," Mary replied tartly.

"Who is this man? What does he do?" asked Alec.

"He's in combinations," Mary said.

Michael snorted laughter. Mary glared at him.

"What's combinations?" Seamie asked.

"Drawers," Michael said.

"Fine undergarments, not *drawers*," Mary countered, an edge creeping into her voice. "He has a factory. Down on Broome Street."

"Oh, does he now?" An edge had crept into Michael's voice, too.

"What's his name?" Alec asked.

"Milton Duffery."

"How old is he?"

"What does he look like?"

"Where does he live?"

Mary, bristling under the barrage of questions, said, "Nell needs a bath tonight. Alec, Ian, don't wait up for me."

Everyone's eyes followed Mary as she walked out of the kitchen. Nell listened, an anxious expression on her face, as Mary's footsteps receded down the hallway. "Where's Auntie Mary going?" she asked plaintively, looking at her father, then at Fiona, then at everyone else, waiting for an explanation as to why the woman she loved most in the whole world had just left. When she didn't get one, she burst into tears.

"Hush, Nell," Fiona said, picking the wailing child up out of her chair. This was Michael's fault. It had to be. She turned to her uncle, her eyes narrowed. "What did you do?"

"*Me?*" Michael said, affronted. "I didn't do anything!"

"Too right," Alec said, a bite to his tone. He folded his newspaper and laid it on the table, then crossed his arms over his chest. "How long must a woman wait?"

"I was only two minutes late!" Michael exclaimed. "And I said I was sorry! What was I supposed to do? Let a hundred pounds of meat go off?"

"I'm not talking about the bloody meat case," said Alec.

"Then what are you talking about?" Michael asked, perplexed.

"Mary looks after Nell as if the bairn were her own. She cleans. Cooks. She spends most every evening with you."

"I pay her for what she does. Is it not enough? I can pay her more."

"Lord God, but you're thick, lad. It's not money she wants. It's *you.*"

Michael sat down heavily, looking as if he'd been knocked sideways. "She...she told you this?"

Alec shook his head. "She didn't. She wouldn't. She's too proud. But she doesn't need to. Anyone with eyes can see how she feels. Well, almost anyone."

Michael put the heels of his hands against the edge of the table, as if he wanted to push it away, and everything else with it—the delicious meal, the people sitting around it, their expectations.

"I-I'm sorry if I gave her the wrong impression, but I'm not...I'm a widower. I'm in mourning. I can't..." he stammered.

"Can't what? Get your head out of your arse? It's been nearly three years. Your mourning's over."

"That's not for you to say," Michael retorted.

"You lost one woman," said Alec. "If you're not careful, you'll lose two." Then he rose from his chair, picked up his plate, and shoveled food onto it.

"Where are you going?" Fiona asked, talking loudly to make herself heard above Nell's howling.

"A man can't eat with all this caterwauling. I'll have my supper in my room tonight."

A moment later, he was walking out of the flat, slamming the door behind him. Ian quickly heaped food onto his own place and trailed after him, not wanting his grandfather to eat alone.

Michael was right behind him.

"Where are *you* going?" Fiona demanded, upset by the exodus.

"For a walk!" he angrily replied.

"But your dinner will get cold!"

"I've lost me appetite!"

A moment later, the door slammed. Fiona bit back a few choice words, not wanting to upset Nell again, whose howls had dulled down to hiccupping sniffles. Fiona put the little girl back in her chair, scooped some mashed potatoes onto a plate, and set it before her. Nell promptly threw it on the floor. Fiona stared at the mess but made no move to clean it up. An unhappy silence had settled over the four people left in the kitchen.

Nick was the first to break it. "*Milton Duffery...*" he mused. "Sounds like a pudding." He picked up his napkin ring and made a monocle of it. "Why, Lady Creakybones, you simply *must* try the Milton Duffery!"

Seamie and Nell giggled. Fiona did not. "It's not funny," she said glumly. "Alec is right; my foolish uncle is going to lose Mary. What are we going to do about it?"

"We shall deal with the Duffery as we would any pudding!" Nick declared. "We shall drown him in custard sauce!"

"*Nicholas.*"

Nick let the napkin ring fall into his hand. He tried to look contrite.

"What if this turns into something?" Fiona fretted. "What if Milton Duffery actually courts Mary? What if he becomes her suitor?"

"Aren't you getting a bit ahead of yourself?"

"Is Mary getting a new suit?" Seamie asked. "I thought she was getting new underwear."

"No, Seamie," Fiona said, putting a drumstick on her brother's plate. "Milton Pudding...I mean *Duffery*...has nothing to do with suits. Eat your supper."

"But you said Milton Duffery is a suiter, Fee."

"How could Michael have let this happen?" Fiona asked, as she scooped mashed potato onto Seamie's plate. "He cares for her. I know he does. It couldn't be more obvious. So why isn't he courting her?"

Nick was quiet for a long moment, then he said, "He can't. He's still married."

Fiona stopped scooping. "What do you mean?"

"He's still married to Molly. He still wears his wedding ring. He still has her photograph in the sitting room. Look around, Fiona..." He gestured to the framed pictures of flowers on the walls, the lace curtains, the pretty vase and teapot and well-worn cookbook standing neatly on a shelf. "He won't let her go."

Fiona followed his gaze, nodding. "You're right. But it's not good. It's not healthy. He has to move on."

"But that's just it—he doesn't have to. Mary is like a wife to him..." He glanced at Seamie, who was gnawing on his drumstick. "...in many ways. Except for one. And he's not ready for that. Not ready to let a woman into his heart again. Not ready to love again."

"But Mary is."

"Apparently. And it seems he's taken her for granted."

Fiona looked at the heaping platter of perfectly roasted chicken, the bowl of fluffy mashed potatoes, the basket of pillowy rolls, then raised her eyes to Nick's and said, "Perhaps we all have."

Chapter 3

Nicholas watched as Seamie ran up the sidewalk with a wooden sword in his hand, startling a flock of pigeons into flight. The boy, all red hair and freckles, was always bursting with pent-up energy when school let out. He was a bright, perceptive child, but he struggled with sitting still at his desk. He lived to climb trees and clamber up rocks in Central Park, and on the rare occasion when he did settle down to read a book, it was always about an explorer.

Soon school would be out for the year, and then he would be off to a sleepaway camp in the Adirondacks. Fiona thought he was too young, but he'd pleaded and begged and nagged until he'd finally worn her down.

"What are you worried about? Are you afraid he won't like it and will want to come home?" Nick had asked, after Seamie had presented Fiona with a list of all the things he would do without being told to—make his bed, brush his teeth, polish his shoes, take out the rubbish—if she would let him go.

"No, I'm afraid he *will* like it," Fiona had replied. "Last night, he recited the names of all the highest mountains in the world and told me he's going to climb every single one. He means it, Nick. The second he finishes his schooling, he'll set off for parts unknown. Do I have to lose him now, at seven?"

Nick, seeing her distress, had refrained from telling her that she was right—that Seamie would love camp. Instead, he'd covered her hand with his own and squeezed it. She had lost too many family members during her young life and had difficulty accepting that her little brother would stretch his wings one day and leave her, too.

That's why they'd stopped at a hardware store after they'd fetched Seamie from school, and why they were carrying paint cans. Because Fiona didn't want to lose anyone else.

Three days had passed since Mary had accompanied Milton Duffery to the concert, and Fiona—anxious to learn just how friendly Mary's new friend was—had found a reason to drop by her uncle's flat the very next day. But Mary had taken Nell to the park, Michael had been in an untalkative mood, and neither Alec nor Ian had anything to share about Mary's outing because she'd told them nothing. Though Alec did say that he suspected Mary had met Milton Duffery at choir practice, and that this affair might've been developing for some time.

"Mary's no fool, Fee," Nick said now. "She'll figure out what we're up to."

"She won't," Fiona said confidently. "We have the perfect excuse. I've come to try out some paint samples and you're helping me."

"But the shop doesn't need repainting."

"That's beside the point," Fiona said. She glanced up ahead and saw her brother about to jump into a puddle. "Seamus Finnegan! Don't you dare!"

"It's meddling," Nick insisted, as Seamie jumped over the puddle. "Mary and Michael are grown-ups. If something needs to be sorted out between them, they're the ones who have to do it."

"It's not meddling, it's helping," Fiona countered. "It's finding a way to talk to Mary about her…about the man…when no one else is around to make things awkward. She works in the shop most afternoons, Nell will be napping, Alec will be digging in the garden, Ian will be making deliveries, and Michael has an appointment with a real estate agent about a warehouse we're interested in. It's the perfect time to find out more about the mysterious Mr. Duffery."

Nick shot her a sideways glance. "I forgot. Meddler is your middle name."

"They're our family, Nick," Fiona said simply. As if those words were enough, as if they explained everything.

They do, Nick thought. *They explain her.*

Nicholas Soames had never known what family truly meant until he'd met Fiona. He'd had one, of course—a father and mother, sisters—but for them, love was a shiny gold star to be earned for good behavior. Fiona had taught him that his family's kind of love—cold and conditional—was no love at all. She'd not only saved his life when he'd fallen deathly ill, she'd saved it again when she'd married him in a courthouse wedding to spare him from prison after he'd been arrested on trumped-up vice charges. She'd fought for him, sacrificed for him, protected him. She'd taught him that love—real love—is anything but conditional. Love is ferocious and enduring, and it is not for cowards.

"Now remember, Nick, don't bring up the outing first thing," Fiona said as they arrived at the shop. "We have to be subtle."

"Hi, Auntie Mary! Where's your new suit?" Seamie bellowed as he opened the shop's door and ran inside.

"So much for subtlety," said Nick.

"New suit? What do you mean, laddie?" Mary asked, stepping out from behind the counter to give the boy a hug.

"You have a suiter. Fiona said so."

Mary tilted her head and regarded Fiona. "Did she now?"

A blush crept into Fiona's cheeks.

"Will it be nice, your new suit? Will it be blue? That's my favorite color."

"Seamie, love, I bet Alec could use some help in the garden," Fiona said.

Seamie looked from Mary to Fiona to Nick, then shook his head disgustedly. "Why do *I* always get sent outside when Fee's the one in trouble?" he grumbled, heading for the back door.

As soon as he was gone, Mary addressed Nick and Fiona, hands on her hips. "And what might you two be shopping for today? Bread? Pork chops? Rumor and innuendo?"

"We're not shopping for anything, Mary," Fiona said, feigning innocence. "We came to try out paint samples." She lifted a paint can high. "I've been wanting to change the wall color in this place for months."

Mary snorted, but before she could say anything further, the shop door opened again, and a man stepped through it.

"Good afternoon, Mrs. Munro," he said.

"Why, Mr. Duffery, what a lovely surprise," said Mary with a smile.

Nick and Fiona spun around so quickly, they smacked their paint cans together, startling the newcomer.

"I don't believe you've met my friends, Mr. Duffery," Mary said. "Mrs. Fiona Soames, may I present Mr. Milton Duffery? Mrs. Soames owns this shop, together with her uncle. And this is Mr. Nicholas Soames, her husband."

Nick put his paint can down on the floor. Fiona followed suit.

"A pleasure Mrs. Soames, Mr. Soames," Milton Duffery said, approaching them.

"The pleasure is entirely ours, Mr. Duffery," said Fiona, forcing a smile.

Nick reached for Mr. Duffery's hand, determined to give him the benefit of a doubt, and found himself face-to-face with a portly man of average height, with light brown hair macassared flat to his skull, a wispy mustache, and owlish eyes behind rimless glasses. Nick guessed he was in his fifties. He wore a three-piece suit of gray worsted, a white shirt with a detachable collar, and a black tie. A gold watch chain was looped across his vest front. What Nick could see of his brown leather shoes was buffed to a sheen; the rest was covered by rubber galoshes. Even though rain was not in the forecast.

"I hope I'm not intruding," Mr. Duffery said, glancing at the paint cans.

"Not at all," Mary replied. "Mrs. Soames was just choosing colors. She wishes to repaint the walls."

Milton Duffery looked around the room, frowning. "Yes, I can see why. The current color is quite dingy." He looked up. "Then again, perhaps that is the fault of the lighting. That is an old gasolier, Mrs. Soames. Replacing it with a new model would brighten the room considerably."

Fiona winced at the criticism. Milton Duffery didn't see it, but Nick did, and the goodwill he'd grudgingly extended evaporated. He picked up his paint can and started to shake it vigorously. "There is nothing that I would rather do, sir, than rid the premises of an old gasolier," he said, looking pointedly at Mr. Duffery.

Fiona shot him a cautioning look. "If you'll excuse us, Mr. Duffery," she said, picking up her own can.

"Of course, Mrs. Soames." He walked toward the counter. Mary was still standing in front of it. "I trust you enjoyed the concert on Saturday evening, Mrs. Munro?"

Mary opened her mouth to reply, but Milton Duffery didn't give her the chance. He kept right on talking. About the program, and how some find Schubert dull, but that he greatly preferred him to Beethoven, to say nothing of Mozart.

"Windbag," Nick said, under his breath.

Fiona elbowed him in the ribs.

Mr. Duffery continued his critique by adding that the cellist was not up to par, the violin section's pizzicato was leaden, and the bassoonist must surely have been suffering from catarrh.

"Pompous ass."

"I did enjoy the lemon squash we shared afterwards. A bit tart for my taste, I must say, but refreshing nonetheless."

"*Shared*?" Nick huffed. "A cheapskate, too."

Fiona pinched him.

Nick had bought two paintbrushes at the hardware store and had stuffed them into his jacket pocket. Fiona pulled one out and walked the length of the shop, searching for a bare patch of wall where she could try out a color. Nick had begun to do the same when Mary stopped him.

"Mr. Duffery, did you know that Mr. Soames is a businessman, too?" she said. "He deals in art."

"I'm in combinations and hosiery, myself," said Mr. Duffery, puffing out his chest. "In fact, I've just launched a new line of sock garters for men."

"Have you? How utterly thrilling," Nick said.

Milton Duffery, blissfully unaware of the sarcasm in Nick's voice, continued. "I call it *Duffery's Smarter Garter*. It employs a softer elastic band that doesn't chafe, and grippier metal clips that hold the sock edge securely without tearing it. However, my newest and most exciting innovation —" He held up a finger. "I'm afraid I must swear you to secrecy, sir…"

"Be not afraid, Mr. Duffery. Be not afraid in the least. All the demons in hell could not make me repeat one word of this conversation. To anyone. Ever."

"*Nicholas!*" Fiona mouthed, glaring at him from behind Mr. Duffery.

"I am glad to hear you say so, Mr. Soames," said Mr. Duffery. "Now, as I was explaining, this product is so new, I haven't even advertised it yet." His voice dropped low, as if he were a spy divulging state secrets. "It's called *Duffery's No-Flap Chin Strap*. It lifts sagging wattles and presses them back into place." He pointed at Nick's neck. "Why, you could use one yourself. I can see the very beginnings of a double-chin. It may have escaped your notice, but it is there,

I assure you. It's easy to wear the device. You simply strap it on before retiring and remove it upon rising. I wear mine with my mustache trainer. To gain the best results, I advise that you wear it every night without fail."

Nick looked at the man as if he had just thrown a dead rat at his feet. "I would rather die, sir," he said.

Fiona sucked in a sharp breath. She hurried to his side and squeezed his arm. "*Try*, sir," she quickly said, flashing Milton Duffery a too-bright smile. "My husband would rather try your brand, than any other. I will buy him one the very instant it's available. Now, come along, Nicholas. I need your help."

As Fiona shepherded Nick over to a wall, Mr. Duffery returned his attention to Mary. "I wish to purchase a few items for my table, Mrs. Munro. Two sausage rolls. Three pork pies. Four currant scones. And that lovely madeira cake."

"I'll wrap them for you right away. Shall I put them on account?"

"Yes, please. You are a fine cook, Mrs. Munro. A very fine cook, indeed. And I can see from the state of this shop that you are a tidy housekeeper, too."

Mary flushed with pleasure. "You're very kind to say so, Mr. Duffery."

"My sister cooks for me and I wish she had as light a hand with pastry as you do. She is too free with the suet. An excess of fat unbalances the digestion, Mrs. Munro. It leads to biliousness and an over-dependence on magnesia." Mr. Duffery shook his head dolorously, then continued. "Her cooking leads to steep dentist bills, too, I'm afraid."

"Does it?" Mary asked. "How so?"

"She is a bit careless, my sister, I don't mind telling you. She wore her favorite ring as she kneaded bread dough last week, you see…"

"A thrilling raconteur, too? My word, is there no end to the man's talents?" Nick whispered, slapping paint on the wall.

"…and unbeknownst to her, the stone dropped out of it. She was beside herself with worry when she discovered it was missing, fearing it was lost forever. Well, I found it, didn't I? That very next morning when I took a bite of toast! Cracked a molar. This one right here…" Milton Duffery hooked a finger in his cheek and stretched it wide. "Oo thee?"

"Yes, I do. How painful that must've been," Mary said.

Mr. Duffery released his cheek. "Such is the bachelor's burden," he sighed.

Mary handed him his purchases, neatly wrapped in brown paper and tied with string.

"Thank you, Mrs. Munro," he said as he took them. "I was wondering…"

"Yes, Mr. Duffery?"

"Might I have the honor of your company at the East Side Temperance Society's Saturday evening singalong? I think you would have a very nice time. We sing only good, clean, old-fashioned songs. None of that racy new rubbish."

Nick turned around. "My word, doesn't *that* sound like fun?"

Mary ignored him.

"There will be a supper afterwards," Milton Duffery continued. "Fried chicken, I'm told. Cookies and sarsaparilla, too."

"I would be delighted to accompany you, Mr. Duffery," Mary said warmly.

"Splendid. I shall call for you at four o'clock." He held up a finger. "*Sharp*. Good day, Mrs. Munro."

"Good day, Mr. Duffery."

"Mr. Soames…Mrs. Soames," said Milton Duffery, doffing his hat as he opened the shop door.

"Good-bye, Mr. Duffery," Fiona said.

"And good riddance!" Nick fumed, as the door closed behind the visitor. He pointed his paintbrush at Mary. "You can't possibly…you don't really mean to—"

"Stop before you start," Mary warned.

"But Mary, he's a—"

"*Stop*," Mary said, sharply enough that Nick flinched. She saw it and softened. "My options are somewhat limited, Nicholas. I am a widow who comes with a teenage son and an elderly father-in-law. I am hardly considered a catch."

Mary looked so vulnerable as she made this admission, that Nick felt a flame of chivalry ignite in his heart. "Rubbish!" he protested. "You are the finest catch in all of New York!"

Mary smiled at his words, but her smile was tinged with sadness. "You are very sweet to say so, but I can't go on as I've been doing."

"Why not?" Fiona asked, concerned. "What's wrong? Have we done something?"

"It was me, wasn't it? Banging on about a Victoria sponge the other night," Nick said, pained by the memory.

"Don't be ridiculous. You've done nothing wrong, either of you."

"Then what is it?" Fiona pressed.

Mary looked down at her hands. "It's…well…" she began awkwardly. "People talk."

"Who's talking?" Fiona demanded. "What are they saying?"

"That it's improper, a widow and widower living in the same building, spending so much time together. *Why buy the cow when you can get the milk for free?*"

Anger colored Fiona's cheeks. "Who said that?"

"Maggie Flaherty."

"Why, that old toad."

"She is an old toad, but even so…it's time. Time I moved on with my life." Mary paused for a moment, struggling with her emotion, then added, "I loved my late husband very much, and I've always heard it said that you only get one big love in your life, if you're lucky. I think it's time I accepted it."

Nick understood what Mary was saying — and what she wasn't.

So did Fiona. "You don't love Mr. Duffery," she said.

Mary polished a bit of imaginary dust off the counter with her sleeve. "It's a bit early to be talking about love, isn't it? And anyway, there are many different kinds of love."

"Yes, there are," Fiona agreed. "Like true love. The kind you feel for Michael."

Mary blushed. And winced. "Right to the point, lass. As always."

"Why don't you tell him how you feel?"

"I can't, Fiona," Mary replied. "I'm not a modern woman like you. I'm rather old-fashioned, I'm afraid. I expect the man to make the first move."

"But Michael —" Fiona pressed.

"Does not return my feelings," Mary cut in. She lifted her head, and Nick saw the depth of her heartache etched upon her face. "Don't you think he would have said something by now if he did?"

Fiona, flustered, stammered an answer. "Well, I…I don't…I mean, he —"

"Exactly," Mary said, then she changed the subject. "I need to run upstairs to check on Nell. Keep an eye on the shop for a minute, will you?"

Nick and Fiona watched her as she disappeared through the doorway that connected the shop with the building's foyer and the staircase to the upper floors.

Then Fiona turned to Nick. Her jaw was hard-set, her gaze intense. "Milton Duffery is moving fast, Nicholas," she said. "He has made inroads."

Nick waved a hand dismissively. "He has taken Mary out once."

"Once that we know of. And he's taking her out again this Saturday."

"I'd hardly call two outings inroads."

But Fiona seemed not to hear him. Worry darkened her eyes. "I don't have a good feeling about this. Mary cares for Michael and he cares for her, I *know* he does, but he's going to lose her if he doesn't make a move."

"I hope you're wrong. I really do. Poor Mary. Can you imagine it?"

"Imagine what?"

"The pudding climbing into bed at night with his chin strap and his mustache trainer and his bottle of magnesia," Nick replied, with a shudder.

"We have to *do* something."

"But what? We can't force Michael to talk to Mary," Nick said, remembering how Michael had stormed out of his flat on Saturday evening after being confronted by Alec. "And it looks like Mary isn't going to approach him, either."

"I don't know what to do. Not yet," Fiona replied. "But I'll come up with something."

"Well, how about we finish splotching paint colors on the walls in the meantime? It's getting on," Nick suggested. He picked up his paintbrush again.

"Yes, let's. Then we'll collect Seamie and go home. I have a fair bit of accounting to do tonight and the sooner I make a start, the better. I'm just going to run up to Michael's flat to get my shawl. I was so upset with him last night, I forgot it."

"Fee?" Nick called after her.

"Mmm?" Fiona said, turning in the doorway.

"Matchmaking is a tricky business. One must tread lightly where hearts are involved."

"When have you ever known me not to tread lightly?" Fiona asked.

Nick snorted laughter.

Fiona leveled her chin at him. "Mary deserves better than Milton Duffery. She deserves her heart's desire. And I mean to see that she gets it."

Then she disappeared through the doorway and Nick heard her footsteps, quick and light, hurrying up the stairs, and his heart clenched painfully with love for her. And with sadness.

"Ah, Fee," he whispered in the silence of the shop.

He knew her. Better than anyone. And he knew that she would fight hard for her friend, determined that Mary would find true love.

Because she herself had lost it.

❧ Chapter 4 ❦

If she squinted, Fiona could see it all again—the squalor, the despair, the grief.

Dirty clothing on the floor. Unmade beds. Crusty dishes in the sink. Spoiled food on the table.

She could feel her ribs tightening around her heart, the panic rising inside her. For a moment, standing by herself in the quiet emptiness of her uncle's flat, it was the spring of '89 again. She and Seamie had just arrived in New York, hoping for a warm welcome, a helping hand. Instead, they'd discovered that their aunt was dead and their uncle was trying to join her by drowning himself in alcohol.

By force of will, and with the help of the Munros, Fiona had managed to save her uncle, and his business, and forge a new family. Nick, Michael, Nell, Mary, Alec, and Ian—they were her family now, hers and Seamie's, and she could not imagine her life without every single one of them in it. It was selfish, her wish to see Michael and Mary wed; she knew it was. But only a little. Most of all, she wished for the happiness of two people she loved. If they lost each other, there would be days—many of them—when they would struggle to convince themselves that what they were living was not a second-best life, pale and sad.

She knew that well enough, for she had lost the one she loved—Joe Bristow, the boy with the whole world in his smile.

They'd grown up together on the same shabby street, she and Joe. They'd planned to marry, and dreamed of opening a shop together. They'd scrimped and saved to make that dream come true, but one drunken night, Joe had made a terrible mistake and had smashed that dream into a million jagged pieces. And Fiona's heart with it. And yet, she still held him inside her broken heart. She still talked to him in her head. Still whispered her hopes and dreams to him as she closed her eyes at night. She knew she would never love any man the way she'd loved Joe.

There are many kinds of love, Mary had said. But Fiona knew she was wrong. There is one kind of love—true love. Everything else is a consolation prize.

"Throw the ball to me, Ian! I can catch it!"

The sound of Seamie shouting carried up from the backyard, shaking Fiona out of her thoughts. It was getting late. Ian was already home from baseball practice. Nick was waiting for her, supper had to be made and served, and her dining table was covered with papers, ledgers, and bills.

Her heart felt as heavy as a brick as she walked into the kitchen. She didn't know how to get Mary and Michael to talk to each other. How to chase Milton Duffery away. How to keep her family together. And what about Saturday's family dinner? Would there even be one? Milton Duffery was taking Mary out again. Who would cook it?

"How do I fix this? What do I do?" she said aloud in the empty kitchen, frustration getting the better of her, but the kitchen had no answer.

Fiona's shawl was right where she'd left it, draped over the back of a chair. She picked it up and was about to settle it on her shoulders when she saw that the clean dishes from last Saturday were still in the drainer and the scrubbed pots and pans were still on the stovetop. She knew that often it was all Michael could do to get Nell fed and bathed and in her bed in a timely fashion, so she set her shawl down again and started to put things where they belonged, hoping it would make her uncle's evening a little easier.

A few minutes later, she was nearly finished and reaching for the last thing in the drainer—an old blue-and-white striped teapot with a chipped spout. It belonged on an open shelf, next to the cookbook, but as Fiona went to put it there, she saw that the cookbook had fallen on its side. She stood it back up and wedged the teapot into place beside it, but as she turned to go, the book toppled over again and smacked into the teapot. She whirled around and barely caught both objects before they tumbled to the floor. Heart thumping, she carefully pushed the teapot back into place with one hand, and pulled the book off the shelf with the other. She would leave it on the table to prevent it from toppling again and rearrange the entire shelf when she had more time. But as she was about to put the book down, the title, embossed in black on the front cover, caught her eye: *Mrs. Beeton's Cookery Book.*

She ran a finger over the words. *You could cook the Saturday dinner*, a voice inside her said.

Fiona shook her head, chuckling at the notion. She had little interest in cooking and even less interest in cookbooks.

To her, balance sheets made for exciting reading, not reci-pes. And hadn't Nick told her just days ago that she was a terrible cook?

"Egregious, actually," Fiona said to herself, her eyes lin-gering on the book.

She was about to put it down when, without quite knowing why, she opened it instead. As she did, her eyes fell on an inscription, written in a spidery hand.

> *14 May 1887*
> *For dearest Molly, on the joyous occasion of her wedding.*
> *With love,*
> *Aunt Margaret*

Fiona caught her breath, moved by the bittersweet dis-covery. The book had been a wedding gift. She pictured Molly and Michael, arm in arm after their ceremony. Setting up their flat. Sharing their first meals as newlyweds. Starting a life together. The young bride who'd unwrapped this book and held it in her hands, her heart so full of happiness, had no idea how short that life would be.

Nick with his paint brushes, Seamie and supper, the mountain of work awaiting her—Fiona forgot them all as she started to turn the pages.

The book had been well-loved. Its edges were bumped, its spine cracked. There were stains and splatters on many pages, and notes scrawled in margins. *Double the cinnamon. Reduce baking time by ten minutes. No garlic for Alec.*

"Molly also cooked for the Munros," Fiona murmured. "They were family then, too."

She kept turning the pages and found recipes clipped from magazines and newspapers tucked within them, as well as advice on growing flowers and easing headaches. There were cheerful poems about tidy homes, old friends, and new babies. There was a business card with *Michael Finnegan, High Class Grocer* printed on it, a ticket stub from Coney Island, a pressed violet, a Valentine's card, a green foil shamrock.

Mrs. Beeton's had been more than a cookbook to Molly, Fiona realized. It had been a scrapbook of the life she had Michael had begun to make together, and Fiona felt that she was getting to know her aunt a little through her notes and keepsakes. She rarely asked Michael about Molly because remembering her made him so sad.

As her fingers skimmed over recipes for consommé, fricasseed chicken, and Lady Baltimore cake, Fiona felt as if Molly were in the kitchen with her, seated at the table, hands curled around a hot cup of tea, urging her to read on.

The clock chimed from Michael's sitting room.

Five o'clock. Nick will be wondering where I am, Fiona thought. She knew she should go downstairs. She didn't budge.

Sausages with onion gravy, lamb and barley stew, shepherd's pie…many of the recipes were familiar to her and brought her back to suppers with her family in London. Her mother and countless other East London women had kept their large broods together by keeping them around the dinner table. On nothing more than a pound a week.

If they could do it, why can't I? Fiona wondered. *All I have to do is choose a few recipes and follow them. How hard can it be?*

"Fee, come on!" a voice bellowed from the doorway. "We're hungry!"

Fiona snapped out of her trance. "Coming, Seamie!" she shouted back. She grabbed her shawl and wound it around her shoulders.

What do I do? she had asked despairingly, just a little while ago.

As she slipped the cookbook under her arm, then slipped out of Michael's flat, she was certain she'd found her answer.

Chapter 5

The nattily dressed salesman standing behind the glass display case in Tiffany's flashed a wide smile.

"Good morning, Mr.—" he started to say.

"Soames. Nicholas Soames," Nick finished.

"Pleased to meet you, Mr. Soames. My name is George. Are you buying for your wife? Or…" he hesitated; his eyes shifted from a pearl necklace to a diamond choker, "…for a sweetheart?"

Nick arched an eyebrow, amused. "Do you mean *mistress*, old sock?" he said. "Haven't got one of those I'm happy to say. From what I hear, they set you back a pretty penny. I'm looking for a gift for my wife, who also happens to be my business partner, trusted advisor, and dearest friend."

"She sounds like a most remarkable woman," said George. "What does she like?"

"Adding machines. Industrial scales. Cash registers," Nick replied. He laughed at George's appalled expression. "Ghastly, I know. Which is why I'm here. Because she deserves a beautiful thing for a change."

"Let us find her one, then," George said, pulling out an emerald brooch. A pair of ruby earrings. A sapphire hair comb. An enameled pocket watch. A garnet choker.

George showed Nick jewel after exquisite jewel, but nothing met with his approval. "Too old," he said, dismissing the brooch. "Too crusty. Too fusty. Too flashy," he added, dismissing everything else.

Half an hour later, an exhausted George stood amidst a king's ransom of glittering gems that Nick had rejected. Then, suddenly, he brightened. "I have just the thing," he said, holding up a finger. "One moment, please, Mr. Soames." He asked a colleague to put the unsuitable offerings away and hurried to the back of the store. There, he unlocked a tall cabinet, extracted a rectangular leather box, then returned to Nick.

"This necklace arrived this morning with a collection of jewelry from the continent. We haven't put any of the pieces out yet," he explained, placing the box down on the display case. "It's for a certain type of woman, one who doesn't follow trends but sets them."

As George undid the clasp and eased the lid back, Nick caught his breath.

Inside the box, nestled on a bed of black velvet, a dragonfly rested on a flowering branch. It was so lifelike, Nick half-expected it to take flight. Its eyes were cabochon emeralds, its body a line of shimmering opals, its weblike wings delicately enameled in a translucent bluegreen. The flower petals were shaped from mother-of-pearl. The branches themselves, cast in gold, formed a collar-like structure. It was an original, elegant and striking. Like Fiona herself.

"It's perfect. Put it on my account," Nick said. He'd seen the price tag. It would eat up every cent of the profits from the Van Gogh sale and then some. He didn't care.

"Very good, sir," said George. He turned to the wooden counter behind him to wrap the box.

Nick smiled, allowing himself to imagine Fiona's reaction as she opened his gift. As he waited for George to finish, a happy din from the shoppers around him drifted to his ears. It was a Friday afternoon and the store was full of people. A giddy teenage girl tried on a bracelet. An older gentleman perused a tray of watch fobs. A young couple picked out wedding rings.

But one voice, gratingly pedantic, rose insistently above all the others, marring the merry hubbub.

"…therefore, in my opinion, sir, what you require is a lighter undergarment. You must try my sleeveless, knee-length union suit. It employs long-staple cotton for breathability with a patented closed-crotch construction and separate front and back openings that allow for superior ventilation. Another important benefit? Roomy, one piece fabrication, which ensures an absence of constriction in the midsection thus alleviating biliousness…"

Nick froze, like a gazelle sensing a lion in the tall grass. He turned his head slowly, eyes sweeping back and forth, scanning the room.

And then he spotted him.

Milton Duffery.

He was standing at a counter, a few yards away, his body turned from Nick at a three-quarter angle. He was talking to a salesman—who was doing his best to hide his mortification—about underwear.

Nick's eyes widened in panic. *I have to get out of here. Right now*, he thought. *Before the Duffery sees me and inquires about* my *undergarments.*

He was about to turn back to George, blabber some fib about a forgotten lunch reservation, and ask him to hurry, when he saw the salesman hand something to Milton Duffery.

It was a ring.

A diamond ring.

Nick's heart nearly skidded to a stop. As he watched, motionless with horror, Milton Duffery held the ring up to the light, pinched between his thumb and forefinger. He examined it, squinting, turning it this way and that, then tucked it into a ring box that was resting on the counter.

"Shall I wrap it for you, sir?" the salesman asked.

"No need," Milton Duffery said, as he dropped the little box into his jacket pocket. "The box will keep it safe until I give it to her."

"Good God," Nick whispered, pressing a hand to his chest. "When, pudding, *when?*"

"Here you are, Mr. Soames. I'm sorry if I took too long," George said, concern on his face. He held out Nick's purchase, now wrapped and tucked inside a pretty bag.

Nick realized George thought his urgent question had been directed at him. "You didn't take too long, George. And you are most definitely *not* a pudding. Must dash," he said, snatching the bag.

Pulling his hat down low over his face, Nick made a run for it, hoping against hope that Milton Duffery did not turn around as he passed by. A few seconds later, he was safely outside the store and hurrying through Union Square.

Fiona had given him an errand to do that morning. She'd made arrangements with Thomas McTaggart, a house painter, to repaint the grocery shop, and she'd asked Nick to drop off the deposit. But it would have to wait. Milton Duffery had just bought a diamond ring. Nick had to find Fiona and tell her immediately. She'd said that Milton Duffery was going to move fast, and he had not believed her, but she was right. They would have to come up with a plan and fast. There was no time to waste.

The threat was real. It was dire.

The pudding could strike at any moment.

꙰ *Chapter 6* ꙰

"Nick, what's the matter?" Fiona asked, rising from her chair.

It was just after two-thirty. She'd been sitting at the dining table in their flat, stealing a quick bite of lunch, when her husband burst into the room, red-faced and breathless. His suit was rumpled. Perspiration glazed his forehead. He held a robin's egg blue bag in one hand.

"Are you unwell? Does something hurt you?" she asked, hurrying to him.

"Yes, something does."

Fear sunk its sharp talons into Fiona. "Should I fetch Dr. Eckhardt?" she asked. "Is it your heart?"

"No, it's my aesthetic sensibilities," Nick replied.

"Nicholas Soames!" she cried, swatting at him. "Don't frighten me like that!"

"May I have some tea? I'm parched," Nick said, kissing her cheek.

A tray was resting on the dining table. It held a teapot, teacup, and a plate of finger sandwiches. *Mrs. Beeton* lay next to it. Nick dropped his bag on the table, sat down, and snatched a salmon and cress sandwich. As he gobbled it, Fiona poured him a bright, fragrant Darjeeling from the pot.

"I should pour this over your head," she said, handing him the cup. Nick's health was delicate. She worried about it constantly. "What happened?"

"I saw the pudding. In *Tiffany's*!" Nick exclaimed, as if he'd spotted a man-eating tiger rampaging through the city.

"Yes, so?" Fiona said, putting the teapot down. She didn't understand why this would upset him so much. And then she did. "Nicholas," she said, her voice heavy with dread. "You don't think —"

Nick gulped a mouthful of tea, then said, "I don't think…I *know*. Milton Duffery bought a diamond ring. I saw him do it with my own eyes. First, he courts Mary. Next, he buys a ring. You're good with equations, old girl. Add *that* one up."

Fiona's blood ran cold. "I told you he was making inroads. You didn't believe me," she said accusingly.

"Well, I do now."

"This is faster than I'd imagined," Fiona added, feeling blind-sided. "They've only just started seeing each other. He's behaving like some love-sick young swain."

"The pudding is not love-sick. Or young. Or a swain. The pudding is a dull and self-seeking pragmatist," said Nick, reaching for another sandwich. "Who hopes to find himself an economically advantageous arrangement—cook, housekeeper, and wife, all in one."

As Nick ate, Fiona sat down across from him, her brows knitted together in solemn concentration. This new development was not good; it would force her hand.

"I'm going to talk to Michael," she said.

"You tried that already."

"I'll try again."

"When?"

"Tomorrow evening. After supper."

"How? We're not having our Saturday supper. Mary's going out with the Duffery. Did you forget?"

"We *are* having supper. I'm going to cook it."

Nick's eyes grew as round at two pie plates.

"Just stop," Fiona said. "It'll be delicious. I borrowed Molly's cookbook." She nodded at *Mrs. Beeton*, lying open on the table.

"And I shall be borrowing Milton Duffery's magnesia."

Fiona glowered at him. Nick ignored her.

"Do you know that he was talking about biliousness again? In Tiffany's!" he said, affronted. "Is it a wife the man wants or a gastroenterologist?"

"What were you doing in Tiffany's anyway?" Fiona asked, glancing at the bag. "You were supposed to drop the deposit off at the painter's."

"I meant to. I did," Nick said, doing his best to look remorseful. "But I ran home to tell you about the pudding instead."

"Oh, Nicholas, you are impossible," Fiona scolded. "I promised McTaggart he'd have half of his money today. What if he takes another job?"

"I'll do it tomorrow."

"And remind him that I asked him to come not this Tuesday, but a week from Tuesday, at five-thirty, after the shop closes. I'm paying him extra to start and finish all in one night, so we don't lose any business.'

"First thing tomorrow, I promise," Nick said. Then his faux-contrite expression melted away and a Cheshire-cat grin replaced it. "Don't you want to know what I bought at Tiffany's?"

"Cufflinks?"

"No."

As Fiona watched him, he reached for the bag he'd placed on the table, pulled out a beautifully wrapped box, and handed it to her. Then he sat on his hands like an over-excited child.

"For you," he said.

Fiona gave him a quizzical look. "For me? Why?"

"Just *open* it, Fee."

Mystified, Fiona carefully removed the ribbon and wrapping paper and set the leather box down on the table. Then she eased the box's lid back and gasped. She shook her head, overwhelmed.

"Is this…this isn't…"

"For you?" Nick said. "Yes, it is. Do you like it?"

"*Like it*? Nicholas, I…I don't even know what to say," Fiona whispered. "It's *beautiful*. It's the most beautiful thing I've ever seen."

"For the most beautiful woman I've ever seen," Nick said. He stood up, lifted the necklace from its velvet bed, and fastened it around Fiona's neck. "There," he said, settling the dragonfly just under the V of her collarbones. Then he leaned back to appraise its effect. "Stunning, old shoe. Go look."

Fiona rose and hurried to the mirror hanging over the fireplace. Her eyes widened at her reflection. Never in her life had she imagined she would own such an exquisite piece of jewelry. She touched the delicate dragonfly. Her eyes met her husband's in the mirror.

"Nick...*why?*"

"To say thank you."

"For what?" she asked, turning to him. "Is this about the Van Gogh? You sold that painting, not me."

"Thank you for loving me, Fee."

"Oh, Nicholas. Of course, I...you don't have to..."

Fiona's words fell away. She wanted to tell him just how much she loved him, and that she always would, and that Vincent van Gogh had nothing to do with it, but a lump rose in her throat and she couldn't talk at all.

"Thank you," she whispered when she finally found her voice again. "But you shouldn't have."

"Yes, I should," he said, and she was surprised to hear that his own voice had turned husky. He touched the back of his hand to her cheek. "Because I love you. And I believe in love, Fiona. Not pragmatism. Not convenience. Not sensible arrangements. *Love.* Everything else be damned."

Fiona thought of the handsome young man Nick had loved, the man he'd lost. Nick still kept his photograph. "Even after everything that happened? After losing Henri?" she asked.

"Yes. Even after everything. Do you regret one moment you spent with Joe?"

"No," Fiona said softly. "I must be mad, but I don't." She squeezed his hand. "Nor do I regret one moment I've spent with *you.*"

"Then you are *definitely* mad."

Fiona laughed and kissed him and the two sat down again, poured more tea, and finished their sandwiches. As he ate, Nick's eyes strayed to the cookbook lying on the table.

"Do you really think you can soften Michael up with a family supper?" he asked, reaching for it.

"I hope so. Mary won't make the first move, so he has to."

"It might just work," Nick said, paging through the book. "But if you are to defeat the pragmatic pudding, you must devise an effective plan of attack. Your battlefield will be the kitchen table, *Mrs. Beeton* will be your general, and Michael's favorite dishes will be your artillery. Now, what does he like best?"

Fiona looked at her husband as he pored over recipes. He had spent all of his earnings on her necklace; she knew he had. And he shouldn't have. They'd both had some measure of success in their business endeavors, but they also still shouldered heavy financial burdens, and he could have used the money to pay down debt or acquire more stock for his gallery. She almost told him so, she almost told him to be pragmatic himself and return the necklace, but she bit her tongue, knowing better than to try to change what she loved about him. Nick seized the bright, beautiful moments in life as a way of defying its darkness, and to ask him to stop would be like asking a butterfly to fold its brilliant wings and turn back into a caterpillar.

He had taught her so many things in the short time she'd known him, but there was one lesson that had lodged deeper in her heart than all the others, one that she would put to use now, as she tried to help Mary and Michael: That win or lose, love is always worth the fight.

Chapter 7

Flushed, sweaty, and covered in flour, Fiona set the platter down on the kitchen table, then stepped back, hands on her hips, a triumphant smile on her face.

Nick, Alec, Ian, Michael, Seamie, and Nell all stared at the thing sitting in the middle of it, expressions of dread on their faces.

Michael was the first to speak. "What is it?" he asked.

"What do you mean, *What is it*?" Fiona retorted. "It's a roast beef!"

Michael shook his head in disbelief. "That's the top round I gave you? Jaysus."

"Mind your language at the table. It's supposed to look like that."

Nick tilted his head, his eyes still on the charred, lopsided lump. "It's supposed to look like a deflated rugby ball?"

"A crusty one?" Seamie said.

"That crust is called a sear," Fiona said knowledgeably. "It locks the juices in."

Ian pointed to the small, dark objects framing the roast. "What are those?"

"Potatoes. What did you think they were?" Fiona asked, returning to the stove.

"Chunks of coal," Ian said, under his breath.

Fiona carried a bowl of soupy creamed spinach to the table, and then a plate of biscuits that were as flat as manhole covers. Nick picked one up and tried to take a bite of it. It was like trying to bite into a slab of marble.

"Um, Fee?" he asked lightly. "I'm curious…did you use baking soda in the biscuits or baking powder?"

"Yes."

"Which one?"

"I can't remember. Aren't they the same thing, roughly?"

Nick hid the biscuit under his napkin. "We're in for it, chaps," he whispered.

Fiona put a gravy boat on the table then sat down herself, still wearing her apron, her shirtsleeves rolled up. She'd worked on the supper for three hours and was excited to finally serve it. She hoped to be able to do what her mother had done. And her Aunt Molly. And Mary. She hoped to make her family and friends feel well fed and cared for, to unite them around the table.

And the meal did unite them. Just not in the way she expected.

"Alec, would you say the blessing?" she asked.

Alec shook his head. "Not me, lass. This is a job for the pope."

Michael shot him a look and he grudgingly put his head down and blessed the food.

When he finished, Fiona handed the carving knife and fork to her uncle. "Would you do the honors?"

Michael eyed the charred joint, took the utensils from Fiona, and took a deep breath. He poked the prongs of the fork into one end of the roast and started to cut, but the blade slipped off the blackened crust. He tried a second time, but it slipped again, clanging loudly against the platter. Frowning, he stood up, and like a safecracker hacksawing his way through solid steel, managed to carve off several dry, stringy slices. He plated them, garnished each with potatoes, then passed the plates down the table until everyone had been served.

Nick served himself a spoonful of spinach, then watched as it oozed across his plate like something scooped from the bottom of a pond. He bravely took a bite, gagged, and smiled.

Seamie attempted to spear a potato with his fork, but it shot off the plate and landed in the gravy boat with a plunk.

Ian attempted to cut his roast beef, but couldn't, so he surreptitiously picked the slice up and tried to tear off a bite with his teeth. He pulled so hard that the meat ripped apart violently and his hand slammed down on his plate, flipping it. It hit the vase of flowers on the table and almost knocked it over.

One by one, the diners put their forks and knives down in silent surrender.

"Fiona, lass, God love you for trying," Michael said, "but the damn thing's inedible."

Fiona exhaled a long, defeated breath, her hopeful expectations for the meal congealing like cold grease. "It is a bit well-done, isn't it?" she said.

Alec's bushy eyebrows shot up. "Well-done? It's incinerated!"

"I'm sure we can salvage it somehow," Nick said stoically.

Everyone else looked terrified at the mere suggestion. They all stared at the spinach in its bowl, now turning a sinister shade of gray, at the gravy with a half-inch of grease floating on top of it.

Alec pushed his plate away. "What's open for supper near here, then?"

"Whelan's Ale House," Michael replied.

"Over my dead body," Fiona said.

Whelan's was where she'd first found her uncle, sunk in grief, drunk and incoherent, after she and Seamie had arrived from London.

"We won't have to go far. Whelan just moved. He's across the street now," Michael said.

"Did he bring his beer kegs with him?" Fiona asked archly.

"It's not the same place it was," Michael assured her. "Whelan got married. To a nice German lass. She cleaned things up. Cleaned Whelan up, too. They have sausages and sauerkraut now."

"Let's go!" Seamie piped up.

Everyone got to their feet except for Fiona. Ian and Seamie pounded down the hallway to the door. Alec was right behind them. Michael hauled Nell out of her chair and followed.

Only Nicholas lingered. "Aren't you coming?" he asked her.

"I'm not hungry."

"Don't be like that, old girl. Come with us," Nick coaxed.

"You go. I'm exhausted," Fiona said, looking around at the colossal mess she'd made.

"Put your feet up," Nick advised, "and don't go near those dishes. I'll help you with them when we get back." As he finished speaking, his stomach let out a long, loud growl.

Fiona gave him a sympathetic smile. "Poor man. Go. Before you starve to death."

As soon as she heard the door close, she rose and attacked the mess. Though she was tired, she wanted to rid the kitchen of all evidence of the evening's catastrophe. First, she scraped everything into the trash, sighing with regret at the waste, then she stacked the dirty dishes, set the pots and pans to soak, and started to scrub.

"How on earth did Mary manage it?" she said aloud, up to her elbows in sudsy water. How had her own mother made delicious, filling suppers night after night after night?

Under Fiona's frustration were darker, harder feelings. She had hoped to remind her uncle how important family meals were, and talk to him afterward about approaching Mary, but she wouldn't get the chance now. She'd hoped to keep things from changing, but she was too late—things had already changed. And even if she learned how to cook like a five-star chef tomorrow, what did it matter? Milton Duffery would soon ask Mary to marry him, and the days of them all crowded around the rickety kitchen table would fade into memory.

An hour later, when everything had been washed, dried, and put away, Fiona decided to join the others at Whelan's. She tried to spark a little hope inside herself. Maybe she could still find a moment to talk with Michael. Maybe she could ask Nick to take Seamie home and walk back here with her uncle on the pretext of some business matter that needed discussing. The important thing was to not let him think she was trying to corner him. Which she was.

Fiona took off her apron, then glanced around the kitchen to make sure she hadn't missed a crumpled napkin or a dirty glass and as she did, her eyes fell on the cookbook, still lying open on the windowsill.

"You have a lot to answer for, Mrs. Beeton," she said, scowling at it. Then she picked it up, meaning to put it back on its shelf, but as she started to close it, a piece of paper slipped from its pages and fell to the floor. She knelt down to retrieve the paper. It was folded in half.

"Where did you come from?" she murmured, puzzled.

When she'd first opened the book, a few nights ago here in Michael's kitchen, she'd turned every page, and examined every memento pressed between them, curious about her aunt, eager to know her better. How had she missed this one?

As Fiona unfolded the paper, she saw that there was no photograph inside it, no ticket stub, or lacy valentine.

There were only words.

And as she began to read them, her hand came up to her heart, and tears came to her eyes.

Chapter 8

"Fiona? Where are you?"

Footsteps echoed down the hall. Michael had returned from Whelan's and was making his way to the kitchen. Fiona, still sitting at the table, was staring out of the window. Michael called to her again, but she didn't answer him. She didn't trust her voice.

"There you are!" he said, walking into the kitchen. He carried a sleepy-eyed Nell tucked up in one arm, and held a plate of food covered with a cloth in his free hand. "Why are you sitting here all alone?" he asked, placing the plate on the table. "That's for you. Sausages, sauerkraut, and a piece of apple cake."

Fiona turned away from the window to face him; as she did, he abruptly stopped talking. His gaze traveled over her face, taking in her red eyes, the silvery sheen on her cheeks.

"Aw, lass. We didn't mean to hurt your feelings," he said. "But you burnt that roast right to shite."

"I'm not crying over the supper, Uncle Michael," Fiona said, wiping her cheeks with her palm.

"What are you crying over, then?"

"This," she said, touching the note she'd found, which was folded up again and lying on the table. "I went to put

Aunt Molly's cookbook away and this fell out of it. It's from her, Uncle Michael. To you."

Michael inclined his head, as if he hadn't heard her correctly. "Fiona, is this some kind of joke? Because it isn't funny."

"It's not a joke. Here," she said, pushing the note across the table. "Read it. I did. I probably shouldn't have, but I did."

Michael sat down at the kitchen table across from her, Nell drowsing on his shoulder, and looked at the note. Fiona could see that he was working up the courage to pick it up, and after a long moment, he did.

She watched his face as he read it. She knew the words by heart now.

My dearest Michael,

I am dying. Dr. Mason will not say so, but I see it in his eyes. God has given me a few moments' relief from the pain, and I am writing my last words while I have the strength to do so. It will be easier for you to read them after I am gone, I think, than to hear them from my lips.

I'm afraid, Michael. Wherever I'm going, it won't be this. It won't be you. It won't be Nell. After such happiness here on earth, what can heaven offer me?

You have given me so much, but there is one final thing I must ask of you—I want you to marry again after I am gone. Find a woman who will love you and will love Nell, too, as if she were her own. Mary Munro is my first choice. She has been like a sister to me and is such a good mother to Ian. And she has been a widow for too long. Some might say that it's strange for a wife to pick out her replacement, but I do not think so. I never knew how much love a heart can hold. Not until I met you. You have the biggest heart, Michael, and there is room enough in it for both of us.

Take good care of our Nell. Tell her about me one day. Tell her how much I wanted her, how much I loved her. Tell her how much I loved her father.

Forever yours,
Molly

After a long moment, Michael folded the note and placed it back on the table.

Fiona looked at him. She couldn't see his face clearly because his head was lowered, but then he spoke, and she heard in his voice what he was feeling in his heart. She heard all the things grief had put there — anger, fear, sorrow.

"The end came quick. She'd been writing, just before…before things got bad. I thought it was a grocery list for a supper she was planning." He laughed. It was a dry, bitter sound. "The doctor must've tucked the note inside her cookbook. She had it with her, y'see. I never opened it after she passed. Couldn't bear to."

It was the most Michael had ever told Fiona about Molly's death, and it cost him; Fiona could see that.

"She knew you," Fiona said, trying to encourage him. "Better than you know yourself. She knew what you would need. Who you would need."

"Time. That's what I need, Fiona. Time."

"You haven't got it."

Michael's hand, resting on the table, knotted into a fist. "Don't start this again, lass."

"I don't want to, believe me. It's not pleasant arguing with you," Fiona said. "But you care for Mary, I know you do. And she cares for you. And Milton Duffery bought a ring yesterday. A diamond ring. In Tiffany's. Nick saw him. So stop being stubborn and listen to me."

"He bought a ring?" Michael asked.

Fiona nodded.

Michael got to his feet. He looked desperate and frightened, like a horse that wanted to bolt. "Take her," he said, handing Nell to Fiona. The little girl, sweaty and sticky and sleepy, mewled in protest.

Anger flared inside Fiona. "I can't believe this. Are you running off again? Where are you going this time?" she demanded, taking Nell into her arms.

Michael grabbed the vase off the table and pulled the flowers out of it, dripping water all over the table. "Out," he replied, leaving the kitchen.

Fiona tried to stand up, to go after him, but the weight of the sleeping child in her arms made her clumsy. She knocked into the table and upset the vase. It teetered back and forth; she only just managed to catch it before it fell over.

"Uncle Michael? Uncle Michael!" she shouted. "Where are you—"

The door to the flat slammed shut.

"Bloody hell!" Fiona swore, sitting down again. Why did he always run from hard things instead of facing them?

Nell, unhappy at being jostled awake, began to cry. Fiona rubbed her back and hummed a lullaby.

Why did Michael take the flowers? she wondered. *Where on earth is he going with them?*

As Fiona heaved a troubled sigh, the clock in the parlor struck the hour—seven p.m. Nell had curled back into sleep, her head against Fiona's chest. She would put the child to bed in a little while, but for now she held her, enjoying the sweet weight of her, her warmth, her little girl smell. Out of all of them, Nell would suffer the most if Mary left to wed Mr. Duffery, and Fiona felt desperate at the very thought. Mary was like a mother to Nell—the only mother she'd ever known.

As Fiona sat, still humming, the golden rays of the slow-setting summer sun filtered through the kitchen window, falling across the floor, the kitchen table, and the folded letter lying on it. The warm light seemed to set the paper aglow, drawing Fiona's gaze.

She stopped humming and reached out her hand. A tiny flame of hope kindled inside her as she touched Molly's letter. She knew now where Michael had gone. And why. Turning her head toward the sunlight, she whispered three words.

"Help him. *Please.*"

Listen to the mockingbird, listen to the mockingbird,
the mockingbird still singing o'er her grave,
Listen to the mockingbird, listen to the mockingbird,
still singing where the weeping willows wave…

Thirty-two earnest voices rose in wan, warbling unison as the members of the East Side Temperance Society sang the last song on the program of their Saturday singalong, hosted by Miss Adelaide Drayton in the shady back garden of her Washington Square townhouse.

And though Mary Munro sang, too, she did so half-heartedly. She did not like "Listen to the Mockingbird." She'd never been able to reconcile the song's cheerful melody with the subject of its lyrics—young Halley, who'd died and was buried in a valley under willow trees—and she wondered now, as she did every time she heard it, if the person who'd written it had actually ever lost a loved one.

"Ah, one of my favorites!" Milton Duffery exclaimed, after the last notes of the song rose and faded.

He drew out a handkerchief and mopped his brow. Then he removed his jacket and draped it over the back of his wicker chair. His exertions wafted the scent of his cologne through the air. Mary could not place it, though it seemed to contain notes of menthol and, strangely, mustard.

"I shall fetch us some lemonade," he said to Mary, then turned to the elderly woman seated at his right. "Miss Drayton, may I bring you a glass, too?"

"Thank you, Mr. Duffery, that would be lovely."

Milton Duffery rose, then made his way toward the refreshments table, leaving Mary sitting with Miss Drayton.

"Such a considerate man," Miss Drayton said.

"Yes, he is," Mary agreed.

Milton Duffery had been most attentive to Mary all evening. He'd introduced her to the other members of the temperance society, found her a seat in the shade, and when supper had been served, he'd squired her through the line, putting a large piece of fried chicken on her plate, selecting a biscuit for her, dishing up generous helpings of aspic and salad.

Generous? Hah. All he's doing is being free with someone else's food! a voice inside her head scoffed, a man's voice, Irish and cheeky. *And if I were you, missus, I'd have handed it right back. Chicken was as tough as tar paper and the biscuit tasted like a cow pat.*

Mary quickly silenced the voice. It had been kind of Milton Duffery to invite her to the singalong, and kind of the other members to welcome her. And if they talked nonstop about the evils of drink…well, what did she expect at a temperance society event? And if everyone was terribly serious and no one ever laughed…well, perhaps that was how people who did not live in Hell's Kitchen conducted themselves. And if their tastes in music tended toward sad and mournful tunes, toward the —

Bloody funereal! the voice cut in. *Jaysus, is this a singalong or a wake?*

"Enough!" Mary hissed under her breath. The voice went quiet, though she wondered how long it would stay that way.

Miss Drayton, slight and straight-backed in a high-necked dress, stared ahead of herself at a late-flowering dogwood. She hummed a few bars of "Listen to the Mockingbird," a blue-veined hand tapping out time on the arm of her chair, then turned to Mary and said, "It's a strange song, is it not, Mrs. Munro?"

"Why, yes, it is, Miss Drayton," Mary said smiling, surprised that her hostess's thoughts mirrored her own. "I've always thought so."

She leaned across the little table between them, the better to hear Miss Drayton. Perhaps she was a kindred spirit. Perhaps their conversation would take an interesting, maybe even uplifting, turn. Mary hoped so. She could do with a bit of cheerfulness.

"It's a deceptive tune," Miss Drayton continued, "what with its jaunty melody, but then again, so are we human beings, are we not? We wear bright smiles and trill that all is well even as our hearts are aching. But what else can we do? The world is so full of disappointments, and our lives are so burdened by hardship and sorrow, that if we cried over every sadness, we'd be dripping tears like rain clouds." She nodded then, as if in agreement with herself. "Snatch what happiness you can. That is my advice, Mrs. Munro. Before it is too late. For we shall soon—every last one of us—be asleep beneath the willows."

Miss Drayton returned her gaze to her dogwood and Mary's smile curdled. She sagged back against her chair, wishing desperately for a belt of brandy.

Mr. Duffery returned with a plate of pale sugar cookies and offered them first to Miss Drayton, then to Mary, then he placed the plate on the table and sat down.

"There are molasses cookies, too, but they appear to be overly spiced," he said to Mary in a low voice, so as not to offend Miss Drayton. "An abundance of ginger late in the day is unwise, Mrs. Munro. It over stimulates the digestion and makes for a sleepless night."

Mary bit into her cookie. It was as dry as sand. As she washed the bite down with a swallow of lemonade, she suddenly found herself deeply, achingly hungry. But not for cookies. For the kitchen table in Michael's flat and the people gathered around it. She pictured them in her mind's eye—Fiona and Michael arguing about warehouses, Nell splattering applesauce on Nick's spotless shirt, Ian and Seamie telling silly jokes, Alec reading his paper, everyone crammed too close together, talking too much, laughing too loudly. They were there in Michael's kitchen right now, together, while she sat here, feeling as if she'd been marooned on a dull and humorless desert island.

Guess the dreamboat turned into a shipwreck, the voice said.

Mary started to scold it again, but was suddenly overwhelmed by a longing so fierce that instead she leaned forward, ready to stand up, make some quick, fumbling excuse, and hurry home.

But before she could, Miss Drayton spoke, eyeing the serving table. "We appear to be out of lemonade."

Her voice, as creaky as the hinges on a coffin, doused the sense of urgency that had come over Mary. *What am I thinking?* she wondered. Rushing off would be unspeakably rude. And how would she explain her sudden appearance in Michael's flat? They would all know that she hadn't enjoyed her evening with Mr. Duffery. Michael would know. She would look pathetic, like a woman without a scrap of pride.

"I'll fetch more lemonade," she said, starting to rise.

"No, thank you, my dear. I shall ask the maid to do it," Miss Drayton replied, waving away Mary's offer. "It will do me good to stand up and move about." She rose with Mr. Duffery's assistance. "Old bones, Mr. Duffery, old bones," she sighed, before tottering off toward a young woman in a black dress and white pinafore who had just emerged from the house with a bowl of fruit salad.

"Poor woman," Mr. Duffery said, as he watched her go. Then he turned to Mary. "I have discovered, by experimenting on myself, that a nightly regimen of alternating mustard plasters with menthol and camphor wraps to be highly effective in alleviating joint discomfort. I have developed a washable, reusable double-layer cotton dressing, applied to a vulcanized rubber backing and secured with elasticized band, and am pursuing a patent. I shall show you the prototype the next time I pay you a visit. Would you like that?"

I guess that explains the menthol smell. And the mustard. Camphor, too? Why, the man's a walking mothball.

"I'd love to see the prototype, Mr. Duffery," Mary said, silencing the voice again.

"Very well," Mr. Duffery said brightly. "I shall make a plan for next week. But it's getting late—it's past seven already. I should get you home." He picked up his jacket from the back of his chair and started to shrug it on, but as he did, something fell out of it. "How careless of me. I should've known that would happen," he said, bending down to retrieve it.

Mary's eyes widened as she saw what it was. A small box. From Tiffany's.

Mr. Duffery, smiling, opened the box and held it out to her. A diamond ring sat nestled in a bed of velvet. The color drained from Mary's face. Her heart knocked against her ribs. *No!* she thought frantically. *He can't be...not now...not here...*

"It's my sister's ring," Milton Duffery said. "Do you remember me telling you that the stone fell out of it into a bowl of bread dough, and that I cracked my tooth biting into it?"

A giddy relief flooded through Mary. "Oh, yes! Yes, of course I remember!" she exclaimed, pressing her hand to her chest. "It's your sister's ring! Your *sister's*."

If Mr. Duffery noticed that Mary was talking a little too fast and a little too loudly, he gave no sign. "I had it repaired and picked it up yesterday," he continued. "They did a good job, don't you think? I put the box in my pocket and promptly forgot about it. So foolish of me. I could have lost it anywhere."

"Very foolish, Mr. Duffery," said Mary. "Do put it back."

Mr. Duffery snapped the box shut and returned it to his pocket. Then he and Mary said their good-byes to the

Temperance Society members and set off to find a cab to take them across town.

Mr. Duffery chattered as they walked, regaling Mary with the many fascinating steps involved in the production of his patented seamless men's socks, and Mary listened, smiling and nodding—but heard nothing. She turned her head toward him every now and again, but she didn't see him. She rested her hand on his arm, but didn't feel him. She saw another man, tall and broad-shouldered, with hair as dark as night and eyes of the deepest blue. It was his voice she longed to hear, his touch she dreamed of.

Aye, and dreams are all you'll ever have, Mary Munro, she said to herself.

Michael had no room for her in his heart; it was still too full of grief for his lost wife. Molly was gone forever, but it was as if she had never left. And yet, sometimes Mary caught Michael looking at her with a certain softness in his eyes, and dared to hope that he cared for her, too. If only there was some way she could tell him that Molly didn't need to go, for she, Mary, was not afraid of ghosts.

But she would not risk baring her feelings only to be told that he did not return them. Her heart had been broken once, when her beloved husband had died in an accident at the freight yards. She had fit the pieces back together as best she could, and had risen above her grief for Ian's sake, but the cracks remained and she would rather love Michael quietly from afar, with her heart whole, cherishing what might have been, than to have it shattered again.

"Ah! Here comes a cab," Milton Duffery said, pulling Mary out of her reverie. He hurried into the street to flag it down, leaving her on the sidewalk.

As she watched him go, she remembered the trepidation she'd felt earlier when she thought he was offering her a ring. One day, he actually might. What would she do if he did?

Snatch what happiness you can, that is my advice, Mrs. Munro. Before it is too late...

A leftover happiness, small and second best—that's what Miss Drayton wanted for her. Should she accept it? What else could she hope for? Fairytale endings, those glittering, impossible happily-ever-afters, were for queens and princesses, not for a widow with a son to raise.

"I have engaged the driver! Come, Mrs. Munro!" Milton Duffery shouted from the street, holding the cab's door open.

Mr. Duffery was not the love of Mary Munro's life and never would be, but he did have some admirable qualities. He was courteous, sociable, and solvent, and that was more than she could say for many men. And he was here, wasn't he? Taking her out. Fetching her cookies and now a cab. As she walked toward him, she realized something else—her fragile heart would always be safe with him, for she would never love him enough for him to break it.

Perhaps Miss Drayton was right. Perhaps it was time to be sensible.

To settle.

For a perfectly nice, deathly dull, mildly mustardy man.

"She's such a sweet girl, Molly. She laughs a lot. And she's so pretty. Just like her mother. Ah, love, how I wish you could see her."

Michael Finnegan stood in the cemetery by his dead wife's grave. The flowers he'd taken from the vase on his kitchen table were resting at the base of her headstone.

"She's so curious about the world. She's got a good appetite, too, and she's growing like a weed. She likes to be in the shop. Thinks it's the greatest fun to watch the cash register open and close. And speaking of the shop, did I tell you we're looking into buying a warehouse, Fiona and me? The business is growing by leaps and bounds…"

Michael was babbling, talking about anything and everything that popped into his head. He kept it up for a good ten minutes, until there was nothing left to say — except for the one thing he'd actually come to say.

"Maybe you already know why I'm here. You always seemed to know what I was going to say ages before I said it. I read your note, Molly. The one tucked in your cookbook. About…about Mary. I never even knew it was there. Fiona found it, just tonight, and…"

His words trailed off as fear overwhelmed him. *Who, exactly, are you afraid of, lad?* he asked himself. *A dead woman? Or your own bloody self?*

He closed his eyes and sucked in a deep lungful of air. "I…I love her, Molly. I do," he said, the words tumbling out of him. "Not the same as I loved you. I'll never love anyone the way I loved you. And I think she cares for me, too. Not the same way she cared for Ian's father, I'm sure, more like a second-chance sort of thing." He ran a hand through his hair. "Jaysus, I'm makin' it sound like a pile of leftovers, like something you find at the back of the icebox, but it's not. It's love, real love. But maybe just a little quieter, a little softer." He smiled. "She loves Nell, too. She's so good to her. I want you to know that. And Nell loves her right back. And it's not right for a little girl to grow up without a mother. Without someone to teach her about dresses and hairstyles and such."

He paused then, trying to swallow the emotion that was rising in him.

"I don't even know if she'll have me," he added. "But if she does, I might not…I might not come as much as I've been doing. It wouldn't be right. But I'll still come sometimes. I'll bring Nell, too. When she gets a little older. I'll tell her about you, Molly. I'll show her pictures. I'll never let her forget her beautiful mother…I'll never forget my first love…"

The tears came then, hot and fast, and there was nothing he could do to stop them. Sometime later, when his chest had stopped hitching and his cheeks had dried, he looked down at his hands, clenched into fists. His wedding ring glinted up at him in the lengthening summer light.

"Ah, Molly. What do I do with this?" he whispered.

It didn't seem right to keep it, but he couldn't just toss it away, either. He remembered that his wife had been buried with her ring and he decided he would leave his ring here, too. With her. The more he thought about it, the more it seemed like the right thing to do. He squatted down and started to work a small hole in the grass at the base of her headstone with his fingers. When he'd dug down a good six inches, he wiped his hands on his trousers, then pulled at his wedding band. He flinched a little at how naked his hand looked without it.

He kissed the ring, and was just about to drop it into the hole, when out of nowhere, a voice shouted, "What on God's green earth are you doing, Michael, you daft lad?"

"Jaysus!" Michael yelped, his heart hammering. He looked around wildly. "*Molly?*"

An instant later, a young woman came into view. She was walking through the cemetery, several yards to his left. His heartbeat slowed a little. He passed a shaking hand over his brow.

"Of course it's not Molly, you great eejit," he whispered to himself.

The woman didn't see him; he was still on one knee. She carried a baby girl on her hip. Two more small children trailed behind her like ducklings. She was the one who'd spoken—she had to be; there was no one else around. A boy, about seven years old, stood a few feet ahead of her on the pathway. Michael guessed he was the Michael she'd been shouting at.

"It's come apart again, Mammy!" the boy hollered, and Michael saw he was holding a shoe in one hand and its sole in the other.

"Take 'em both off," the woman said wearily as she caught up to him. "We'll fix it when we get home."

Dublin, Michael thought, as he listened to her voice. *With a little New York mixed in. A few years off the boat now.*

The boy did as he was told, and Michael saw that he had no socks on his pale feet. The family walked on, then stopped at a small, plain headstone not far from Molly's. Michael could see them clearly, but they had not noticed him. Remembering his task, he looked down at the hole he'd dug, but before he could bury his ring, something drew his eyes back to the woman.

Her children's faces were all scrubbed. Their clothing was patched but clean. They were wiry, but there was a little bit of meat on their bones. The mother, though…she had dark smudges under her eyes and hollows in her cheeks. Her shoulders poked up under her thin cotton blouse.

Michael knew what was going on. He'd seen it before. In Hell's Kitchen. In London. And long ago, back in Ireland. A mother didn't eat so her children could.

The woman lined her brood up around the headstone, then said, "C'mon on now and say a prayer for your daddy."

A widow, Michael thought. *Can't be more than twenty-five.*

The children pressed their hands together. They bowed their heads.

"Dear God, our daddy was a very good daddy…" one began.

The others quickly chimed in.

"He loved us very much."

"He loved hotdogs, too."

"With sauerkraut and mustard."

"Dear God, can you please see to it that our Daddy gets extra hotdogs for his supper tonight? With chipped potatoes on the side?"

"What kind of prayin' is this?" the woman scolded. "Askin' God for hotdogs!"

"Mammy, can we pray for some hotdogs for ourselves, too? I'm hungry."

"No, we cannot. God doesn't just rain down hotdogs, does He? And in the middle of a cemetery, no less!"

"Why not? God can do anything He likes. Remember Jaysus and the loaves and fishes? Everyone was hungry, and then *Poof*! *Presto-chango*! Plenty to go 'round."

"Michael McGowan, I'd like to remind you that Jaysus is your lord and savior, not some street-corner magician. Now say a prayer for your poor Daddy. A proper one!"

The children started again, and the woman watched them, nodding and listening, straightening a collar, tucking a tendril of hair behind an ear. Tears shone brightly in her eyes as she did, but by the time her children finished their prayers, she had blinked them away.

Michael, who'd been watching them the whole time, suddenly nodded as if he'd heard something. Or someone. He stood up, tamped the dirt he'd dug up down with his toe, and made his way over to the woman.

"Excuse me, Missus," he said quietly, not wanting to startle her.

She quickly turned around, a worried expression on her face. "Were we makin' too much noise? I'm so sorry..."

"Not at all," said Michael. "I just wanted to...well, here..." He held out his ring.

The woman looked at it, then she looked up at him as if he'd lost his mind. "I can't take that," she said, shaking her head.

"Yes, you can." Michael gently took her hand, turned it over, and placed the ring on her palm. As he closed her fingers around it, he bent close to her and in a low voice said, "What happens to that lot if you end up six feet under, too? Go to O'Dowd's pawnshop. Eighteenth and Tenth. They'll give you decent money for it. Use it to buy food. Eat some of it yourself."

"Thank you," the woman said, flinching a little under his scrutiny.

It was painful when people saw the things you tried hard to hide; Michael knew that well enough. Touching the brim of his cap, he took his leave.

"Wait!"

He turned around, a questioning look on his face.

"This ring…was it yours?"

"Aye, it was."

The woman gave him a sad smile, one that said she understood. "You are very kind. I wish there was something I could do for you in return."

Michael jammed his hands in his pockets and looked at the sky. He thought about asking Mary to be his wife. He imagined himself going down on one knee and actually asking her, and he felt his heart quail. Fiona said Mary cared for him, but did she still? After stepping out with Milton Duffery, with his underwear factory, and his fancy concerts, and his diamond ring from Tiffany's?

"There is something, missus," he said, looking at the young woman again.

She nodded earnestly. "Anything."
"Have those kiddies say a prayer for me, too."

Chapter 11

"I'm sorry that took so long, Mrs. Munro!" Milton Duffery said as he joined Mary inside the vestibule of her building. "The cab driver was slow to make change. That's how they try to get a bigger tip out of you, you know."

"Is it, Mr. Duffery?"

"I'm afraid so," he said, making no move to leave, his jacket folded over his arm. "Is it always so dark in here?" he asked, squinting. He looked up at the sputtering light fixture. "Ah. Another aging gasolier. That explains it."

"I don't know how many times I've asked Michael to replace that fixture," Mary said with a sigh. "He never seems to get around to it."

Mr. Duffery nodded. He frowned. He shifted from one foot to the other, then suddenly leaned forward, craning his neck like an ostrich and startling Mary so badly that she backed away from him before she realized he was trying to kiss her.

"I'm sorry, Mrs. Munro," he said, mortified. "I did not mean to offend you. I only thought—"

"No, no, it's quite all right, Mr. Duffery," Mary said, flustered. "I just...I wasn't expecting—"

"I was too forward. Do forgive me. I do not wish to press unwanted attentions upon you."

"I am not offended, Mr. Duffery. Truly, I am not."

"I am relieved to hear it, Mrs. Munro," said Mr. Duffery, as he nervously shifted his jacket from one arm to the other. "You are a very attractive woman, Mrs. Munro, and I—"

His words were cut off by a small, sudden clunk, followed by a metallic ping.

"Oh, no. Oh, dear!" he exclaimed.

"Did you drop something?"

"My sister's ring," he replied anxiously.

"*Again?*"

"I'm afraid so," he said, bending down to pick up the ring box. But as he straightened, they both saw that the box had sprung open and that the ring was not inside it.

"What will I do, Mrs. Munro? My sister will be so angry with me," Milton Duffery lamented. "It was our mother's ring. It means the world to her."

"Don't lose heart, Mr. Duffery. I'm sure it's here somewhere," Mary soothed. "It's so hard to see anything in this terrible light. Let's both look, shall we?"

Slowly, they moved across the floor, bent over, eyes sweeping side-to-side. They peered into corners and along baseboards. They poked under the coat rack and moved a small table but could not find the ring.

"What if it fell into a crack between the floorboards? Or down a mousehole?" Milton Duffery fretted.

He draped his jacket over the banister and got down on his hands and knees. Mary joined him and they redoubled their efforts, crawling across the floor, sweeping their hands out in front of them, poking their fingers into knotholes.

Just when Mary was starting to lose hope, Milton Duffery let out a victorious whoop.

"Here it is! I have it!"

"Oh, thank goodness," Mary said. "Where was it?"

"Wedged into a crack by the newel post. No wonder we didn't see it."

Mary stood, eager to get off the hard floor. As she did, Milton Duffery, winded and flustered, rose to one knee and held the ring out to her.

"My eyes aren't very good in this light. Is it all right, Mrs. Munro?"

Relieved that it had been found and eager to assure the worried Mr. Duffery that all was well, Mary took the ring and nodded.

"Yes, Mr. Duffery!" she exclaimed, smiling.

Just as the words left her lips, she heard the front door creak. She turned toward it, but no one was there. And yet the door was slightly ajar.

"That's strange," she murmured. Perhaps Mr. Duffery failed to close it all the way and a breeze had pushed it open. She took a step toward it, meaning to close it, but a grunt from Mr. Duffery stopped her. He was trying to pull himself up on the newel post, huffing and puffing so heavily that Mary felt obliged to help him.

"It appears Miss Drayton isn't the only one with old bones," he said as he straightened. "I shall employ several of my joint wraps tonight." He retrieved his jacket from the banister and put it on.

"I'm so relieved that you didn't lose the ring," Mary said. "Get it home safely and give it back to your sister before it tumbles out of your pocket again."

"I certainly will," Milton Duffery said, as he tucked the ring box back into his pocket. "Good night, Mrs. Munro."

And then he leaned in close and fumblingly kissed Mary on the mouth. His lips were soft and moist. A cloud of menthol and mustard enveloped her. As he pulled away, she forced a smile and stifled a sneeze.

"Goodnight, Mr. Duffery," she said. "Thank you for a lovely outing."

Milton Duffery gave her a shy nod and then he was gone. As Mary watched the door close behind him, a shudder ran through her. The kiss had been so damp, so chilly, it was like kissing a wet rag. If that's how his kiss felt, what would the rest of the business be like?

No one was perfect, and she was prepared to overlook flaws in a man, knowing full well that she had a few of her own that needed overlooking, but was it so wrong for a woman to long for a real kiss? The kind that took your breath away and made your heart pound? The kind that led to a stolen hour in a sunlit room with his clothing and yours tangled up on the floor?

Wrong or not, it was what she wanted, and though her head urged her to follow a practical course, her heart would not be reasoned with. It might be a fragile and damaged creature, but it was also an insistent one, and it refused to settle for a life without love, without the promise of a sunlit room.

"Well, that's it then, isn't it?" she whispered to herself in the gloom of the entryway.

She would call it off with Mr. Duffery the next time they met. It wasn't right to encourage affection when she did not return it, and she was certain now that she could never love him, not even a little. His kiss had decided her. After she had broken things off, she would move out of Michael's building. She wouldn't stay here any longer, wishing for things that were never going to be.

It would be hard to take herself away from the man she did love.

But not as hard as it was to be near him.

Chapter 12

Fiona could barely contain herself. Two hours had passed since Michael had left the flat, flowers in his hand, and he still wasn't back. Nick had taken Seamie home, Ian and Alec had gone upstairs to their own flat, and she'd stayed behind to look after Nell.

She sat in Michael's living room now, flipping through the pages of a magazine, too agitated to read any of the articles, waiting for him. As she did, she thought about her aunt's letter, awed by the courage it had taken the dying woman to write it. Molly had not thought about herself in her final hours, only her husband and child. Her greatest fears had been for them, and she had wanted only one thing as her life ebbed away: to know that they would be loved.

Molly had known what love is. She'd known it isn't the grand, show-boating gesture; the soaring aria; the duel fought at dawn. It's something else, something quiet and faithful and steadfast. It's someone up early, cooking you eggs. It's a bunch of wildflowers when there's no money for roses. A jacket carefully mended. It's someone to help figure out who to pay first—the landlord or the coal man.

The sound of the flat's door opening got Fiona to her feet. She tossed her magazine onto a table, started toward the hallway, then stopped. *Better not pounce on him*, she cautioned herself, and sat down.

Her uncle's footsteps sounded in the hallway. They were heavy and slow. The instant he entered the room, she jumped up again.

"You were gone so long," she said, anxiously noting the slump in his shoulders, his knotted hands.

"Aye, I went to the cemetery," Michael said, avoiding her eyes. "I needed to talk to Molly before I talked to Mary."

Fiona nodded; she understood. Michael had gone to his wife's grave out of love and respect. He'd gone to say thank you. And goodbye. An ember of hope, small but bright, glowed inside her. "And did you talk to Mary, too?" she asked gently, determined not to spook him. "What did she say?"

Michael, his head lowered, looked up at her. "She said yes."

Fiona's eyes lit up. She clapped her hands; she couldn't help it. "She did? She said *yes*?"

"Aye, Fiona, she did…to Milton Duffery."

Fiona's hands fell slowly to her sides. "I-I don't understand," she said, the fragile ember fading.

"When I got back from the cemetery, just as I was about to step inside, I heard voices in the entryway. Two of them. And then I saw Milton Duffery ask Mary to be his wife."

"No. *No*," Fiona said, shaking her head. "I don't believe you. You're wrong, you must be."

"He was down on his knee, giving her a bloody ring!" said Michael, his voice rising. "And she took it. And said yes. Do you believe me now? I almost embarrassed the shite out of me'self. Only just managed to back out of the doorway in time."

Fiona felt as if her legs had been taken out from under her. "I-I can't believe he proposed to her already," she said woodenly. "Nick saw him buy the ring, but I thought…I thought he would wait for a little while. A month, a few weeks. It happened so fast."

Fiona's worst fear had just come true: Mary would wed Milton Duffery and move out of her uncle's building — and out of his life. Michael was stubborn, gruff, and contrary, but a good man, and he loved Mary and had finally worked up the courage to tell her so. He'd readied himself to take a chance at a new love, a new life, and just as he reached for it, it was snatched away.

Fiona looked at him now. He seemed smaller. Hollowed out. "I'm sorry, Uncle Michael," she said, hurting deeply for him.

"So am I. But it's over and done with now," he said, "and it's time you let it be. Time you let *me* be. And Fiona…"

"Yes?"

"Do not say a word about this to Mary or Ian or Alec until they say something to you. It's Mary's news to share when she sees fit."

Fiona assured him that she would not.

"Good," he said, then he started down the hallway that led to the flat's bedrooms. "I didn't give Nell her goodnight kiss. I'll do that, then I'll get you a cab."

"There's no need. I can walk."

"Not alone. Not at night," Michael said, in a tone that brooked no further argument.

As Fiona waited for her uncle, her eyes fell on the framed photograph of Molly that still stood on a small round table. She picked it up. Her aunt was dressed in her wedding gown, holding a bouquet of roses. Her beautiful face was radiant, but her expression was serious, her gaze hauntingly direct.

Nick's words came back to Fiona as she met that compelling gaze. *I believe in love, Fiona…Everything else be damned…*

"I want to believe, too, Aunt Molly," she whispered, "but it's so hard. Love is supposed to make you whole, but sometimes it rips you apart instead and scatters the pieces."

Love had torn away pieces of Fiona's heart. One lay in a London cemetery with her parents and sister. Another floated on the Thames, where her brother Charlie had drowned. And on the north bank of that broad river, at the bottom of a set of old stone steps, another piece was buried in the mud where it had fallen the day Joe left her.

Fiona wanted to believe that love didn't end. She wanted to believe that the love her parents had felt for her and for Seamie endured. That the love Molly held in her heart for Michael and Nell outlasted death as well. She wanted to believe that love stayed, visible in the lines of a lost letter or the stitches of an old quilt, echoing in the notes of a lullaby, alive forever in the memory of a smile.

"But does it?" she asked her aunt. "Or is that just a pretty tale that fools tell themselves?"

Sighing, she put the photograph down and walked into the kitchen to fetch her purse. *Mrs. Beeton* was where she'd left it, lying on the table, Molly's letter folded next to it. She tucked the letter inside the book, then put the book back on the shelf.

It would stay there now, its pages unturned, its recipes unused, the letter inside just a sad prologue to one more love story that would never be written.

Chapter 13

Nicholas yawned. He stretched extravagantly, then wedged his feet under Fiona's bum.

"Do you mind?" she said, staring at a clutch of paint swatches fanned out across the ottoman.

"Not in the least."

"They're cold," Fiona fretted, shifting a little so that she could lift Nick's feet into her lap and rub them. "Why are your feet always so cold?"

"You know what they say, Fee…cold feet, warm heart."

"Do they?" she absently asked, her attention still on the swatches.

Nick frowned. Fiona looked as if she hadn't slept. There were dark smudges under her eyes. Her cheeks were wan, her mood subdued. He decided to see if he could jolly her out of it.

"Do you know what else they say? Cold feet, devastatingly handsome face. Cold feet, sparkling wit. Cold feet, godlike physique. Cold feet—"

"Modest and humble personality," Fiona finished, shooting him an arch look.

Hmm, Nick thought. *This is going to take a bit more effort than I anticipated.*

They were curled up on the overstuffed couch in their sitting room. The day was cloudy and unusually chilly for June, and Fiona had made a fire. The room was comfortable and beautiful, furnished elegantly but simply, so that nothing competed with the artwork. Nick had picked out the furniture and the fabrics himself. He'd selected a warm white color for the walls and had hung several of his favorite works on them—paintings by Van Gogh, Monet, Pissarro, and Seurat.

"Is there anything better than a lazy Sunday afternoon?" he asked now, trying again to engage Fiona.

"A profitable Monday morning," she replied.

Nick rolled his eyes at that conversation-killer. "What are you doing with those colors, anyway?" he prodded.

"Trying to decide on a paint color for the shop."

"But I thought you had."

"I thought so, too, but now I'm worried that it's too dark. I have to get it sorted out before the painters start." She turned and looked at him. "You *did* drop the deposit off…"

"Of course I did. They're coming on Tuesday after the shop closes. Just as you requested."

He leaned forward and looked at the swatches, about to ask her which color she preferred, but his words were cut off by a shout. It was muffled somewhat by the windows, but still quite loud.

"En garde, pirate scum! It is I, Captain Seamus Finnegan of His Majesty's navy!"

"Why is he in the backyard?" Nick asked.

"I banished him," Fiona said. "He broke another vase this morning practicing his fencing. That's the third one this week." As she spoke, she rubbed her left temple, wincing slightly.

Nick saw it, and decided to take the direct route. "What's the matter, Fee? Tell me. You haven't been yourself this past week."

Fiona sank into the crook of the sofa's curved arm and leaned her head back against it. "Same thing that's been the matter ever since Milton Duffery appeared on the scene," she said, staring up at the ceiling. "Michael…"

"…and Mary," Nick finished.

He remembered how Fiona had returned home from Michael's flat in tears last Saturday. When she'd told him what had happened, Nick had felt his own eyes sting with sadness. He'd never expected that Fiona would fail at her plan to unite Michael and Mary; she so rarely failed at anything. He hadn't known what to do then to make things better, and he didn't know now. Milton Duffery had offered Mary an engagement ring and she'd accepted it. What else was there to do?

"We could always kidnap the Duffery and send him off in a hot air balloon," he ventured, trying for a laugh. "And hope that it crashed someplace far away."

"It wouldn't, though," Fiona said glumly. "He's so full of hot air himself, he'd keep it aloft and make his way back."

"Do you know what's strange about all this?" Nick said, his brow wrinkling. "An entire week's gone by, and Mary still hasn't told any of us about the engagement. Don't you think that's odd?"

"No, I don't. Because she doesn't love Milton Duffery, Nick. She's resigned to him," Fiona said disconsolately. "Do you remember when William McClane asked me to marry him? Do you remember the ring he gave me?"

"Certainly do," Nick said. "It was a jolly great carbuncle of a thing."

"I didn't put it on at first. I kept it in its box. It never seemed meant for me, even after I started to wear it. Not because it was ugly, but because I didn't love the man who gave it to me." Fiona raised her head. Her eyes found his. "Michael and Mary missed their chance. And now it's too late." Fresh tears threatened; she blinked them away.

Nick's heart clenched. He hated for Fiona to be unhappy, more than anything in the world. "Maybe it's not too late. Maybe I could give it a go," he said. "I could try talking to Mary or Michael."

"I don't think it's a good idea. You were right and I was wrong. You scolded me for meddling back when we first found out about Milton Duffery and I should have listened to you. Instead, I barreled ahead and got Michael's hopes up and now he's heartbroken and it's all my fault."

"You only tried to help, Fee," Nick said, taking her hand. "To make things better for two people whom you love very much."

"And instead I've made things worse," Fiona said with a sigh. "Maybe it's time to learn my lesson and stop meddling once and for all."

As the words left her lips, they heard a loud, startling crash, and then the sound of tinkling glass.

Fiona shook her head, incredulous. "How does he do it? How does that boy *always* find something to break?" She stuffed her feet into a pair of slippers lying by the sofa and stalked out of the living room. "Seamus Finnegan!" she bellowed, pounding down the stairs. "The better not have been the back window!"

Nick watched her go, a heavy sadness settling over him. He wanted to tell her that he'd been wrong, and she'd been right—one *should* meddle. He wanted to tell her that if she hadn't meddled when she arrived in New York two years ago, Michael would by lying in a gutter, drunk. He would have lost his shop, his entire building. Nell would have lost her father, the Munros their home. And he himself? He would have lost his life.

They were all here, all well, all together, because Fiona cared enough to yell and cajole and prod and nag and fight for the people who mattered to her.

A log tumbled noisily in the grate. Nick looked at the fire and thought about adding another. Instead, he remained where he was, his gaze fixed on the flames, his fingers softly drumming on the sofa's back. After a moment, his brow smoothed and he nodded, as if he'd come to a decision.

"Perhaps you are right, old girl. Perhaps one shouldn't meddle in others' affairs," he said quietly. And then he smiled. "But when have I ever done what I should?"

$\curlyvee$ *Chapter 14* $\curlyvee$

Whenever Nicholas Soames pictured his conscience, he saw a thin, stoop-shouldered man with small round glasses, tufts of gray hair sprouting at the sides of his head, and tightly pursed lips. The man was sitting at a tall clerk's desk, poring over a thick ledger that contained all of Nick's wrongdoings.

Nick saw him now. *This is a most perfidious deception, Nicholas Soames,* he was saying, wagging a bony finger. *A vile duplicity.*

"Get stuffed, old boy," Nick told him.

A job needed to be done. Honesty and forthrightness had not accomplished it, so now it was time to see what guile and trickery could do.

A small brass bell tinkled as Nick entered the premises of Thomas M. McTaggart—Painter and Wallpaperer. It was Monday afternoon, and he was hoping to catch McTaggart before he closed for the day.

McTaggart, he soon saw, was all the way at the back of his shop, cleaning brushes in a metal sink.

"Good afternoon, sir!" Nick called to him, fording his way through rolls of wallpaper, bags of paste, and cans of paint.

McTaggart shut off the water and turned around, wiping his hands on his paint-splotched coveralls. "Good afternoon, Mr. Soames. What can I do for you?" he asked.

"I was wondering…could you possibly come paint the shop on Wednesday night instead of tomorrow?"

"But your missus told me to come on Tuesday. She was very clear about it."

Nick gave the man his most ingratiating smile. "Yes, I know. But there's been a slight change of plan, you see, and now we need you to come on Wednesday instead."

McTaggart frowned. He pushed his white cap up and scratched his head.

"Of course, you will be compensated for the inconvenience," Nick hastily added.

McTaggart grudgingly agreed to Nick's request, and Nick thanked him. His next stop was Finnegan's Grocery itself. When he arrived there, he paused at the door for a few seconds to steady himself. He needed to be at his most convincing for this, the next part of his plan.

"Hello, Mary," he said as he breezed inside. "How are you today?"

Mary's face broke into a smile when she saw him. "Nicholas! What a lovely surprise! I haven't seen you for days. What brings you here?"

"I had a meeting nearby," Nick said lightly. "I finished early and remembered that Fiona asked me to pick up some coffee. Could I get a pound, please?"

"Of course you can. I've bags weighed out and ready to go. Let me wrap up a few molasses cookies for Seamie, too. They're his favorite."

"Did you hear about our culinary catastrophe last Saturday?" Nick asked.

"Alec mentioned it, yes," Mary said, as she handed him his coffee. "It does sound like Fiona tried very hard, though."

"Yes, she did," Nick allowed. "And how did your evening go? You went to a sing-a-long, didn't you? Did you have a nice time?"

"Oh, I had a lovely time," Mary replied.

Nick's eyes flicked to Mary's left hand as she wrapped Seamie's cookies. It was bare.

Fiona was right. Mary had accepted Milton Duffery's proposal out of resignation, not love. The realization emboldened Nick. What he was doing…it was a bit more than meddling, if he was being perfectly honest with himself, but it was still the right thing to do. Absolutely.

Mary handed him his goods. He thanked her and asked if Michael was in.

"Yes, I heard him go upstairs a little while ago," Mary replied. "He's been out all day. Haven't seen hide nor hair of him."

He's avoiding her, Nick thought. *He doesn't want to see Milton Duffery's ring on her finger.*

"Glad he's in," he said. "Need to ask him something." He started to walk through the doorway between the shop and the building's vestibule, then suddenly turned around, snapped his fingers, and said, "Oh! I nearly forgot. Fiona asked me to remind you that the painters are coming Tuesday evening…that's tomorrow, isn't it?…at five-thirty."

"Yes, I know," Mary said. "She told me several times."

"Well, you know how she is. Likes to double-check things," Nick said with a stagey chuckle. "But you'll be here to let them in?"

"Yes, of course. I'll close at five, and then I have to run upstairs and start the supper, but I can easily be back downstairs by five-thirty."

"Perfect!" Nick said. "Thank you, Mary."

And then he was bounding up the stairs to Michael's flat. "Hello? Anyone home?" he called out cheerily, as he pushed the door open.

"In here!" Michael called back.

Nick followed the sound of Michael's voice and found him sitting at the kitchen table, hunched over invoices. At the sight of him, Nick's smile faltered. Tall and well-built, Michael always seemed to fill up any room he was in. But today he looked thinner, the lines in his face deeper, his eyes duller, as if something vital had drained out of him.

Something has, Nick thought sorrowfully, but then he reminded himself that he had a job to do, and propped his smile back up.

"Where's our darling Nell?" he asked.

"In the yard with Alec," Michael replied. "What can I do for you?"

"I need a favor," Nick said, sitting down in the chair next to Michael's. "I was supposed to give McTaggart the remainder of his payment. But I missed him just now. His shop's locked up," he fibbed, pulling an envelope from his breast pocket. "He's coming tomorrow…Tuesday."

"Aye, lad. I do know my days of the week."

"It never hurts to clarify," Nick said. "Would you mind meeting him downstairs and giving this to him? At five-thirty?"

"That shouldn't be a problem," Michael replied. "I have a meeting with my estate agent, but it finishes at five. I should be back in plenty of time."

"Wonderful! You've saved my bacon," Nick said. He slapped the envelope down on the table, nattered on about the weather, then took his leave.

As he strode east toward his home on Gramercy Park, he couldn't suppress a smug grin. Michael and Mary weren't the only ones who would be at the shop tomorrow. He would be, too. Not actually in the shop itself, but very close by. In Whelan's, at a table by the window, enjoying a cup of coffee and a big piece of Mrs. Whelan's delicious apple cake. From that vantage point, he'd be able to see into the window of Finnegan's Grocery and watch his plan unfold. He knew everyone's schedule. Ian played baseball with his team in a nearby ballfield on Tuesday afternoons. Alec took Nell there in the pram to watch him. Seamie had his fencing lessons, and Fiona accompanied him. Nobody would be around to throw a spanner into his carefully calibrated works. And when Michael and Mary found themselves alone together in the shop, without the noise and commotion that always seemed to attend life at 164 Eighth Avenue, they would at last be able to talk.

Michael had given up. So had Mary. Even Fiona was resigned to the Duffery's triumph. But he, Nicholas, would persevere and save the day.

"It's a bold plan, old boy, and a brilliant one," Nick said to himself. "Tomorrow evening, the pudding will be sent packing and true love will triumph. What could possibly go wrong?"

$\backsim$ *Chapter 15* $\sim$

Seamie stood in the middle of the sidewalk, a fencing foil in his hand.

"But *why* do we have to leave lessons early?" he demanded, jutting his chin.

"Because I'm worried I chose the wrong color for the shop walls and I want to see how it looks before the painters get too far along," Fiona explained. "Come on, will you?"

"I bet D'Artagnan never had to leave *his* fencing lessons early," Seamie grumbled.

"Can you please stop dragging your feet? It's going to pour any minute."

Fiona was hurrying Seamie up Eighth Avenue. It was the dingy walls of the fencing master's studio that had convinced her once and for all that the shade she'd chosen was too dark. She'd cut Seamie's lesson short by fifteen minutes to make sure they got to the shop in time.

It was just after five when they arrived. The shop door was locked, and there was no sign of McTaggart and his crew. Fiona had her own key and just as she put it into the lock, the skies opened.

"Whew! We made it just in time," she said to Seamie as she hurried him inside. "Mr. McTaggart won't be happy with me for the last-minute change, but maybe he can run back to his shop and lighten the paint while his men move things out of the way."

"En garde!" Seamie shouted, brandishing his foil at his reflection in the glass front of the meat cooler.

As Fiona peered at the paint samples she and Nick had daubed onto the walls nearly two weeks ago, the shop door opened. She turned and was surprised to see her husband standing there, but her surprise immediately gave way to concern. She hardly recognized him. He was always so beautifully groomed and dressed. But now his hair was askew. He was wearing no jacket and had a napkin tied around his neck. His face was a picture of panic.

"*Nicholas*? You look as if you've escaped from a lunatic asylum! What's going on?" she asked. "What are you doing here?"

"What are *you* doing here?" Nick demanded, tearing the napkin from around his neck and shoving it into his pocket. "You're supposed to be at Seamie's fencing lesson!"

"I-I came to meet the painters," Fiona replied, taken aback by his tone. "I decided to change the color after all."

"No!"

"*No*?"

"You can't be here. You have to leave. Right now!"

"Nicholas Soames, what on earth is going on? Where are the painters? They're supposed to be here." She put her hands on her hips and gave him a dire look. "You *did* forget to give McTaggart his deposit, didn't you? And now he has canceled."

Before Nick could answer, Ian walked into the shop from its back door, followed by Alec and Nell. They were all shaking rainwater off themselves.

"Uncle Nick!" Nell shouted, happy to see him.

"What…no!" Nick cried. "No, no, no, no, no! *You* can't be here, either!"

Nell laughed, thinking Nick was playing some funny new game.

"But we live here," Ian said, perplexed by Nick's strange behavior.

"You're supposed to be at a baseball game!"

"It looked like rain so the officials called it off," Ian explained. "I practiced bunting in the backyard instead with Grandad and Nell."

Nick groaned. He pressed his hands to his cheeks.

Alec's eyebrows shot up. "What ails you, lad?" he asked.

"The pudding!" Nick replied. The words came out louder than he'd intended and made them all jump. Except for Nell, who clapped because pudding was her favorite.

Alec looked at Fiona. "I think we should fetch a doctor," he said to her in a low voice. "He's unwell. He's raving about dessert."

Seamie had stopped fencing with his reflection and had drawn near. "You mean Milton Duffery?" he asked.

Alec's eyes narrowed as he heard the name. "What's this got to do with him?"

"Surely, you don't need me to tell you," Nick said impatiently. "The proposal? The diamond ring?"

"*What*?" Ian and Alec said at the same time.

"She hasn't told you?" Nick said.

"No, she has not," said Alec. He glanced at his grandson. They both looked as if they'd been hit by a train.

"For goodness' sake, Nicholas," Fiona said, glaring at him. "Mary should be the one to announce the news, not you."

"I didn't mean to!"

"That still doesn't explain why you don't want us here," said Alec.

"Yes, well, desperate times call for desperate measures. And so I did some...some *things*," Nick said, glancing at the shop's clock. It was twenty-three minutes past five. Michael and Mary would be here any minute.

"What kind of things?" Fiona asked, suspicion coloring her voice.

"I told the painters to come tomorrow night. But I asked Mary to come down to let them in tonight, and Michael to come at the same time to pay them."

"Let me guess...neither knows the other one is coming," said Fiona.

Nick nodded. "I was hoping that if they had five minutes alone, they could talk and perhaps save themselves from making a big mistake."

"Nicholas, you have gone too far," Fiona said. "You really have."

"That's rather rich coming from you," Nick retorted.

Alec came to Nick's defense. "He hasn't gone far enough, lass," he declared. "Mary cannot marry that man. Not when she loves Michael."

"What do we do?" Ian asked.

"Come with me to Whelan's. We'll hide out there while they meet here," Nick said. He raced to the door, grabbed the handle, then stopped short. "Oh, no. Oh, blast!" he said, pointing. "Look!"

Michael was half a block away, crossing the street, and holding an umbrella. He didn't see Nick and his co-conspirators—he was too busy watching the traffic—but he would shortly; he was heading straight for the shop.

"Don't panic! Nobody panic!" Nick nearly shouted.

"*You're* panicking!" Fiona shot back.

Alec took charge. "If we can't go out, we'll go up."

"Where? To your flat? Mary's up there," Nick babbled.

"Not to our flat. To Michael's," Alec said. "We'll have to be very quiet so she doesn't hear us on the stairs."

"Brilliant idea! Let's go!"

Fiona took Nell's hand, and the entire group hurried out of the shop, through the open doorway, and into the vestibule. Nick led the way up the stairs, treading as lightly as he could. The others followed him. They were halfway up the staircase when a door opened above them.

It was Mary. She was making her way across the landing.

Everyone froze. Nick felt his stomach plunge. It was over. They were done for. In seconds, she would reach the top of the stairwell and see them.

And then a tea kettle whistled. They all heard it.

"Goodness, where is my head today?" Mary said with an exasperated sigh. Her footsteps receded.

The instant she was back in her flat, Nick did an about-face. "Back to the shop!" he whisper-shouted.

"But Michael will see us!" Ian whisper-shouted back.

"Not if we hide! Go!"

They all hurried back down the stairs as quickly and quietly as they could. Nick brought up the rear. Just as he reached the vestibule again, he heard Mary re-emerge on the landing.

"Gogogogogo!" he hissed, herding the others along.

When they were all back inside the shop, he glanced out the window. Michael had made it across the street and was only yards away now. All he had to do was look up and he'd see them. Then someone called to him from the sidewalk, and he stopped and raised a hand in greeting.

"Broom closet!" Nick whispered to Alec.

Alec nodded and hurried toward it. Ian went with him. Mary was well down the staircase now. Her footsteps were getting louder.

There was a large round display table in the middle of the shop's floor, covered by a long linen tablecloth. Nick lifted it. "Fiona! Under here!"

Fiona, who was still holding Nell's hand, ducked under the table and pulled the little girl with her.

Nick glanced out the window again. Michael was chatting with Tommy Whelan. There was a clap of thunder; the rain started to come down harder. Nick knew the conversation wouldn't last much longer. He grabbed Seamie's hand and was just about to dash behind the counter with him, when he heard a little voice rising from under the table. "One...two...three..."

Nell, he thought frantically. *She thinks this is hide-and-seek. If she's not quiet, she'll give us away!*

Fiona whipped the tablecloth up. "Give me a piece of candy!" she mouthed at him.

Nick scanned the shop. He didn't know where the candy was. He didn't see any cookies, either. Then something colorful caught his eye — a strawberry sponge cake with pink icing. It was sitting on top of the display table. Mary hadn't put it away yet. He grabbed the whole thing, plate and all, and thrust it at Fiona. She took it from him and let go of the cloth.

Mary reached the bottom of the staircase. "Oh, I hope the painters are on time," she said wearily. "I'm in no mood to wait on them tonight."

Nick, his heart slamming, grabbed Seamie and pulled him behind the counter.

They ducked down just as Mary walked in from the vestibule.

And Michael opened the shop door.

Chapter 16

"Oh!" Mary said, pressing her hand to her chest, startled. "It's *you*, Michael."

"Sorry," said Michael, shaking rain off his umbrella. "I didn't mean to startle you."

"You didn't, not really. It's just that I'm certain I locked the door," Mary said, confusion in her voice. "Ah, well, I'm distracted today, I guess. At least I remembered to come down and let the painters in."

"I'm supposed to pay them," Michael said, closing the door and leaning his umbrella against the wall.

There was a mirror hanging on the wall behind the counter. Nick, sitting on the floor, his knees up under his chin, Seamie by his side, could see everything that was happening in it.

Mary crossed her arms over her chest awkwardly. "Did you see him by any chance? McTaggart? On your way in?"

"I didn't, no. Can't for the life of me understand why Fiona's suddenly got to repaint the place. Walls look fine to me."

Mary gave him a rueful smile. "I think I know why. Mr. Duffery expressed the opinion that the color was dingy and I fear she took his words to heart."

"Ah. Mr. Duffery."

"Yes. Mr. Duffery."

A leaden silence descended. Michael walked to the counter and feigned interest in a box of cigars on top of it. Opening it. Straightening the cigars. Then taking one out and tapping it on the counter. Nick prayed that he didn't look in the mirror or decide to step behind the counter. He glanced at Seamie and held a finger to his lips. Seamie did the same.

After what seemed like an eternity, Michael spoke again, still fumbling with the cigar. "Talking of Mr. Duffery, I suppose congratulations are in order."

"Are they?" Mary said with a puzzled laugh. "What's he done?"

Michael looked taken aback. "Well, I-I mean…" he stammered, flustered. "Your engagement."

Mary tilted her head. "My what?"

"I know you haven't gotten around to telling us yet," Michael said haltingly, "but…well, we know and we're all very happy for you."

"Michael, I don't—"

"I know you don't, Mary," Michael said. "Believe me. I wouldn't appreciate it either if someone knew my business before I told them about it. I…I saw you. I overheard a bit, too. The other night, I mean, when you came in with Mr. Duffery. I was coming in from a…from a walk, and I opened the door a little. Before I saw you. I didn't mean to earwig, I swear it. I hotfooted it back down the sidewalk the second I twigged what was going on."

"What, exactly, did you overhear?" Mary asked, her confusion deepening.

Michael colored a little. "Mr. Duffery's…his proposal."

"I have no idea what you're talking about," Mary said. Then she gave a little gasp and flushed crimson. "Oh, you stupid, stupid man!"

"Hold on a minute…"

"I did *not* get engaged."

"But Mr. Duffery gave you a ring."

"He did not."

"But he was down on his knee…"

"Because he was crawling around on the floor, looking for it!"

"Looking for what?"

"A ring!"

"So there was a ring. And you said yes."

"I said yes when he asked me if the ring was all right. The poor man was beside himself. He dropped his sister's diamond ring and thought he'd damaged it."

"His *sister's* ring?"

Mary explained to Michael exactly what had happened.

"So you're not engaged?" Michael asked, when she'd finished, a bit of life returning to his voice.

"No, Michael, I am not engaged. Nor am I likely to be. I've broken it off with Mr. Duffery. Just yesterday, in fact, if you must know."

"But I thought—"

"Yes, well, that's what happens when you mind other people's business!" Mary said, her voice rising with indignation. "Why were you sneaking around by the door anyway?"

"I wasn't *sneaking*, t'ank you very much! It's me own bloody house! Surely, I'm allowed to walk where I like in me own house?" Michael's voice was rising now, too.

Nick grimaced. This was not how it was supposed to go.

Michael paced to the window and looked out of it. "Where the devil are those bloody painters?" he growled.

"Look, I'm glad you're here, Michael," Mary said tersely, "because there's something I need to tell you…"

"What?"

"I'm…I'm going to look for a new flat. For myself and Ian and Alec. I can't stay here."

"Why not?"

"Pride, I suppose. I can't stay where I'm not wanted."

"*Not wanted?* Whatever gave you that daft idea?"

"It's not daft. There's no room for me here, Michael. We both know it."

Michael held up his left hand. As if he were a policeman halting traffic.

Mary looked at him in shock. "Stop? Is that what you're telling me, Michael Finnegan?" she asked, bristling. "Stop what? Stop talking? You want me to be quiet now?"

Nick's heart plunged. Things were going from bad to worse.

"No! I'm showing you my hand, Mary. My left hand. I'm telling you that I took my wedding ring off. I gave it away."

Mary didn't say anything, but Michael must've heard something in her silence, or seen something in her eyes, for he kept talking.

"Mary…I…well, look…oh, Jaysus, here goes. Don't leave, Mary. Please. Stay here. Nell…she'll miss you if you go."

Mary was quiet for a long moment, then she said, "And you, Michael, would you miss me?"

"You know I would."

"No, I do not."

Michael snapped the cigar in half and threw it on the counter. "Ah, damn it all to hell, woman. You're going to make me say it, aren't you? I love you, Mary Munro. And I want you to be my wife. I haven't got a real ring. Not yet. But I'll buy you one. A nice one. First thing tomorrow. In the meantime, this'll have to do." He pulled the foil ring off the cigar he'd mangled and got down on one knee. Then he took her hand and slid the ring onto her finger. "Will you have me, Mary Munro? Will you marry me?"

Nick caught his breath. He was waiting on tenterhooks. He knew they all were—Ian and Alec, Fiona and Seamie and Nell. Waiting. Hoping. Not daring to exhale until they heard that one little word, soft and breathy. *Yes.*

And finally it came, one word. But it wasn't soft and breathy. It wasn't little. And it wasn't yes.

"HURRRRRRRRRRRRAY!"

Seamie, unable to control himself for one second longer, shot out from behind the counter, his sword raised high, yelling at the top of his lungs.

"Hurray! Hurray! Hurray! Hurray!"

Mary shrieked.

"Holy Jaysus!" Michael shouted. He jumped to his feet, lost his balance, and fell backward into a crate of eggs. They exploded under him in a string of staccato pops.

"Seamus Finnegan, what in blazes are you doing down here by yourself?" he yelled, struggling to get up. "Where's your sister?"

Seamie bounded over to the table and yanked the cloth up. "Here she is!"

Fiona smiled sheepishly. She waved. Her hand was covered with pink icing.

Nell, sitting next to Fiona, was dripping in it. Icing was all around her mouth, stuck to hair, plastered to her dress. She was clutching a large chunk of cake in her hands. She laughed when she saw Seamie. "Olly olly oxen free!" she shouted.

Michael did not laugh. "Fiona, what are you doing under there?" he thundered, wiping egg off his backside.

"I…um…I just—"

"You were *spying*," Michael said.

"I was not!" Fiona protested. "I was just…waiting for the painters!"

"Under the bleedin' table?"

"Mum, say yes."

The voice, muffled and disembodied, carried into the center of the room.

Michael looked around, incredulous. "There's more of youse in here?"

"For the love of God say *something*, woman," came another muffled voice. "Before we suffocate!"

Muttering a few choice words under his breath, Michael strode to the broom closet and yanked the door open. Alec and Ian blinked at him from inside it. "Come out of there!" he demanded. "Is that the lot of you? No. Wait…we're missing—"

"Tell him you'll have him, Mary. He's a mess without you," said Nick, climbing out from behind the counter.

"A *mess*?" Michael echoed, glowering.

"Say yes, Auntie Mary," Seamie begged. "Don't marry a pudding! Marry Uncle Michael so Fee stops cooking!"

"Marry a *pudding*?" exclaimed Mary. "Seamie, what are you —"

"Children!" Nick said, smiling brightly. "Where do they get these things?"

"From you!" Seamie said, highly aggrieved. "You said Milton Duffery sounds like a pudding! You said we should drown him in custard sauce!"

"Milton Duffery is a decent man, Nicholas," Mary scolded. "He doesn't deserve to be called a pudding."

"That's debatable," Nick countered. "It's also beside the point. What do you say, Mary? What's your answer?"

For a long moment, Mary, who looked as if she'd just stepped off a roller-coaster, said nothing. Her silence unnerved Nick. He'd hoped to make things right. To save the day. What if he'd ruined it instead?

Nick glanced around the shop, taking in the faces of all the people there. Faces full of hope. They wanted this, too. So much. It wasn't just Michael and Mary who had lost someone they loved; every single person in the room had — a first love, a parent, siblings, a son — and inside each of them was a heart that had been broken.

Nick thought of those hearts now. Time and courage and faith had glued the pieces back together, but they would shatter again, and his would, too, if Mary said no.

Desperation got the better of him and he started to babble. "This probably isn't the sort of romantic, flowery proposal a woman dreams about, is it, Mary?" he said, with a nervous laugh. "What with cake all over the floor, and smashed eggs, and one child yelling like a pirate and another covered in icing, and people popping out from closets and counters and underneath tables and…"

Alec, who'd moved close to Nick, nudged him with his shoulder. "Hush, lad," he whispered.

The elderly man had seen something Nick hadn't—that Mary wasn't listening to him. Her gaze was on Michael now, who was still standing by the broom closet, egg dripping off him. His hands were clenched at his sides. His eyes were filled with uncertainty. He looked achingly vulnerable.

Mary walked up to him as if Nick and the others weren't in the room, as if Michael were the only one there. She took his hands in hers, and then she smiled, and as she did her face shone with a radiance so soft and beautiful, it seemed as if morning sunlight had spilled into the room.

"Yes, Michael," she said. "With all my heart, *yes*."

A cheer went up. Nell joined in, looking as if she didn't quite know why. Seamie raised his sword high. Alec and Ian grinned from ear-to-ear. And Nick sagged against the counter as a happy relief flooded through him.

"I wish we had champagne!" Fiona exclaimed, as she crawled out from under the table, bringing Nell with her.

"We do! I put a bottle of Bolly in Michael's icebox weeks ago," Nick said. "Meant to toast myself, but now we can toast Michael and Mary, *and* me!"

"But I'm hungry," said Seamie.

"I've a ham in the oven. It's big enough to feed us all," Mary said. "I'll just need to do some potatoes…maybe some quick biscuits and peas."

"We shall do the potatoes," Nick declared. "And the biscuits and the peas. It's high time we all pitched in with the cooking. All of us except for Fee, that is."

Fiona made a face at him. "Aren't you a funny boy," she said, as everyone else laughed.

Michael picked up his sticky, crumb-covered daughter. Then he offered his arm to Mary and the three headed upstairs, followed by Seamie, Ian, and Alec.

Fiona stayed behind to clean up the broken eggs. Nick helped by sweeping up the cake crumbs. When they were finished, Fiona locked the shop door. Nick waited for her, unable to resist a bit of triumphant crowing. "We did it, old girl," he said. "Our meddling saved the day. Mine was rather more effective than yours, you must admit. But you did make some important contributions."

Fiona dropped the key into her purse, then turned to him, the evening light slanting in through the door across her face, and he saw not the joyous grin he was expecting, but a pensive wistfulness.

"Is it wrong to feel bad for Milton Duffery?" she asked him.

Nick loved her then, even more than he already did. It was just like her to feel sorry for the old windbag.

"I suppose not," he allowed. "I suppose that even I feel a bit doleful on his behalf, but keep in mind that we saved the Duffery from making a mistake, too. Even a pudding should have someone who truly loves him. His perfect woman is out there somewhere. One day he'll find her and they'll live biliously ever after."

Fiona smiled. And then a single tear slipped down her cheek.

Nick took her hand in his. "What's wrong, Fee? Why aren't you happy?"

"I am happy, Nick," Fiona said, leaning her head on his shoulder. "I'm happy for Michael and Mary, truly. I'm just a little sad, too. For Milton Duffery. And Molly. And Mary's husband. And…" Her voice caught.

Nick knew that she was thinking of her family, too. And Joe. And his own lost Henri.

"I know, Fiona, I know," he whispered, bending his head until it touched hers. "That's the hard thing about love. It ends one day. And there's nothing we can do about it. People leave us. Or are taken from us. But it doesn't matter how love ends, does it? All that matters is that love begins."

ABOUT THE AUTHOR

Jennifer Donnelly is the bestselling, award-winning author of fourteen novels, including the three books of the epic *Tea Rose Saga*: *The Tea Rose*, *The Winter Rose*, and *The Wild Rose*.

Jennifer's work has garnered numerous awards, including a Carnegie Medal, the *Los Angeles Times* Book Prize, a Michael L. Printz Honor, and has been named to numerous best-of lists from retailers, librarians, schools, and literary organizations.

Her books have been published worldwide, with her novel *Stepsister* appearing in 22 global markets. Five of her novels—*Stepsister, Poisoned*, and her three-book *Rose Saga*—have been optioned for motion picture development.

Connect with Jennifer on Instagram, X/Twitter, and Facebook @jenwritesbooks or join her mailing list at www.jenniferdonnelly.com.

www.ingramcontent.com/pod-product-compliance
Lightning Source LLC
Chambersburg PA
CBHW020045310726

48970CB00007B/2423